A Nasty Piece of Work

of Work

AND OTHER GHOST STORIES

LANCE SALWAY

A Nasty Piece of Work

AND OTHER GHOST STORIES

Illustrated by Jeremy Ford

CLARION BOOKS

TICKNOR & FIELDS: A HOUGHTON MIFFLIN COMPANY

NEW YORK

For Glenys and Stuart Carter

Clarion Books
Ticknor & Fields, a Houghton Mifflin Company
Text copyright © 1982, 1983 by Lance Salway
Illustrations copyright © 1983 by Jeremy Ford

'Such a Sweet Little Girl' was originally published
in a collection of ghost stories called 'Ghost after Ghost'
edited by Aidan Chambers and published by Kestrel Books, London.
First published in Great Britain in 1983 by Patrick Hardy Books
First American Edition 1985

Library of Congress Cataloging in Publication Data
Salway, Lance.
A nasty piece of work and other ghost stories.

Contents: Such a sweet little girl—Mother's little
helper—Silver and Son—[etc.]
1. Ghost stories, English.   2. Children's stories,
English.   [1. Ghosts—Fiction.   2. Short stories]
I. Ford, Jeremy, ill.   II. Title.
PZ7.S1554Nas   1985   [Fic]   84-17641
ISBN 0-89919-360-9

Q   10   9   8   7   6   5   4   3   2   1

Contents

Such a Sweet Little Girl

It was at breakfast on a bright Saturday morning that Julie first made her announcement. She put down her spoon, swallowed a last mouthful of cornflakes and said, 'There's a ghost in my bedroom.'

No one took any notice. Her mother was writing a shopping list, and her father was deep in his newspaper. Neither of them heard what she said. Her brother Edward heard but he ignored her, which is what he usually did. Edward liked to pretend that Julie didn't exist. It wasn't easy, but he did his best.

Julie tried again. She raised her voice and said, 'There's a ghost in my bedroom.'

Mrs Bennett looked up from her list. 'Is there, dear? Oh, good. Do you think we need more marmalade? And I suppose I'd better buy a cake or something if your friends are coming to tea.'

Edward said sharply, 'Friends? What friends?'

'Sally and Rachel are coming to tea with Julie this afternoon,' his mother said.

Edward gave a loud theatrical groan. 'Oh, no. Why does she have to fill the house with her rotten friends?'

'You could fill the house with *your* friends, too,' Julie said sweetly. 'If you had any.'

Edward looked at her with loathing. 'Oh, I've got friends all right,' he said. 'I just don't inflict them on other people.'

'You haven't got any friends,' Julie said quietly. 'You haven't got any friends because no one likes you.'

'That's enough,' Mr Bennett said, looking up from his paper. There was silence then, broken only by the gentle rumble-slush, rumble-slush of the washing machine in the corner.

Edward chewed a piece of toast and thought how much he hated Julie. He hated a lot of people. Most people, in fact. But there were some he hated more than others. Mr Jenkins, who taught Maths. And that woman in the paper shop who'd accused him of stealing chewing gum, when everyone knew he never touched the stuff. And Julie. He hated Julie most of all. He hated her pretty pale face, and her pretty fair curls, and her pretty little lisping voice. He hated the grown-ups who constantly fluttered round her, saying how enchanting she was, and so clever for her age, and wasn't Mrs Bennett lucky to have such a sweet little girl. What they didn't say, but he knew they were thinking behind their wide, bright smiles, was: poor Mrs Bennett with that lumpy sullen boy. So different from his sister. So different from lovely little Julie.

Lovely little Julie flung her spoon on the table. 'I *said* there's a ghost in my bedroom.'

Mrs Bennett put down her shopping list and ballpoint in order to give Julie her full attention. 'Oh dear,' she said. 'I do hope it didn't frighten you, darling.'

Julie smiled and preened. 'No,' she said smugly. '*I* wasn't frightened.'

Edward tried to shut his ears. He knew this dialogue by heart. The Bennett family spent a great deal of time adjusting their habits to suit Julie's fantasies. Once, for a whole month, they had all been forced to jump the bottom tread of the staircase because Julie insisted that two invisible rabbits were sleeping there. For a time she had been convinced, or so she said, that a pink dragon lived in the airing cupboard. And there had been a terrible few weeks the year before when all communication with her had to be conducted through an invisible fairy called Priscilla who lived on her left shoulder.

And now there was a ghost in her bedroom.

Try as he might, Edward couldn't shut out his sister's voice. On and on it whined: ' . . . I was really very brave and didn't run away even though it was so frightening, and I said . . . '

Edward looked at his parents with contempt. His father had put down the newspaper and was gazing at Julie with a soppy smile on his face. His mother was wearing the mock-serious expression that adults often adopt in order to humour their young. Edward hated them for it. If he'd told them a story about a ghost when *he* was seven, they'd have told him to stop being so silly, there's no such thing as ghosts, why don't you grow up, be a man.

'What sort of ghost is it?' he asked suddenly.

Julie looked at him in surprise. Then her eyes narrowed. 'It's a frightening ghost,' she said, 'with great big eyes and teeth and horrible, nasty claws. Big claws. And it smells.'

'Ghosts aren't like that,' Edward said scornfully. 'Ghosts have clanking chains and skeletons, and they carry their heads under their arms.'

'This ghost doesn't,' Julie snapped.

'Funny sort of ghost, then.'

'You don't know anything about it.'

Julie's voice was beginning to tremble. Edward

sighed. There'd be tears soon and he'd get the blame. As usual.

'Come now, Edward,' his father said heartily. 'It's only pretend. Isn't it, lovey?'

Lovey shot him a vicious glance. 'It's *not* pretend. It's a real ghost. And it's in my bedroom.'

'Of course, darling.' Mrs Bennett picked up her shopping list again. 'How are we off for chutney, I wonder?'

But Edward wasn't going to let the matter drop. Not this time. 'Anyway,' he said, 'ghosts don't have claws.'

'This one does,' Julie said.

'Then you're lying.'

'I'm not. There *is* a ghost. I saw it.'

'Liar.'

'I'm not!' She was screaming now. 'I'll show you I'm not. I'll tell it to *get* you. With its claws. It'll come and get you with its claws.'

'Don't make me laugh.'

'*Edward!* That's *enough!*' His mother stood up and started to clear the table. 'Don't argue.'

'But there isn't a ghost,' Edward protested. 'There can't be!'

Mrs Bennett glanced uneasily at Julie. 'Of course there is,' she said primly. 'If Julie says so.'

'She's a liar, a nasty little liar.'

Julie kicked him hard under the table. Edward yelped, and kicked back. Julie let out a screech, and then her face crumpled and she began to wail.

'*Now* look what you've done,' Mrs Bennett snapped. 'Oh *really*, Edward. You're twice her age. Why can't you leave her alone?'

'Because she's a liar, that's why.' Edward stood up and pushed his chair aside. 'Because there isn't a ghost in her bedroom. And even if there is, it won't have claws.' And he turned, and stormed out of the kitchen.

He came to a stop in the sitting-room, and crossed over to the window to see what sort of day it was going to be. Sunny, by the look of it. A small tightly cropped lawn lay in front of the house, a lawn that was identical in size and appearance to those in front of the other identical square brick houses which lined the road. Edward laughed out loud. Any ghost worthy of the name would wither away from boredom in such surroundings. No, there weren't any ghosts in Briarfield Gardens; with or without heads under their arms; with or without claws.

He turned away from the window. The day had started badly, thanks to Julie. And it would continue badly, thanks to Julie and her rotten friends who were coming to tea. And there was nothing he could do about it. Or was there? On the coffee table by the television set there lay a half-finished jigsaw puzzle. Julie had been working on it for ages, her fair curls bent earnestly over the table day after day. According to the picture on the box, the finished puzzle would reveal a thatched cottage surrounded by a flower-filled garden. When it was finished. If . . .

Edward walked across to the table and smashed the puzzle with one quick, practised movement of his hand. Pieces fell and flew and scattered on the carpet in a storm of coloured cardboard. And then he turned and ran upstairs to his room.

He hadn't long to wait. After a few minutes he heard the sounds that he was expecting. The kitchen door opening. A pause. Then a shrill, furious shriek, followed by loud sobbing. Running footsteps. A quieter comforting voice. Angry footsteps on the stairs. The rattling of the handle on his locked bedroom door. And then Julie's voice, not like a seven-year-old voice at all any more, but harsh and bitter with hate.

'The ghost'll get you, Edward. I'm going to tell it to get you. With its claws. With its horrible, sharp claws.'

And then, quite suddenly, Edward felt afraid.

*

The fear didn't last long. It had certainly gone by lunchtime, when Edward was given a ticking-off by his father for upsetting dear little Julie. And by the time Julie's friends arrived at four, he was quite his old self again.

'The ugly sisters are here!' he announced loudly as he opened the front door, having beaten Julie to it by a short head.

She glared at him, and quickly hustled Sally and Rachel up the stairs to her room.

Edward felt a bit guilty. Sally and Rachel weren't at all ugly. In fact, he quite liked them both. He ambled into the kitchen, where his mother was busy preparing tea.

She looked up when he came in. 'I do hope you're going to behave yourself this evening,' she said. 'We don't want a repetition of this morning's little episode, do we?'

'Well, she asked for it,' Edward said sullenly, and sneaked a biscuit from a pile on a plate.

'Hands off!' his mother said automatically. 'Julie did *not* ask for it. She was only pretending. You know what she's like. There was no need for you to be so nasty. And there was certainly no excuse for you to break up her jigsaw puzzle like that.'

Edward shuffled uneasily and stared at the floor.

'She *is* only seven, after all,' Mrs Bennett went on, slapping chocolate icing on a sponge cake as she did so. 'You must make allowances. The rest of us do.'

'She gets away with murder,' Edward mumbled. 'Just because she's such a sweet little girl.'

'Nonsense!' his mother said firmly. 'And keep your mucky paws off those ginger snaps. If anyone gets away with murder in this house, it's you.'

'But she can't really expect us to believe there's a ghost in her bedroom,' Edward said. 'Do *you* believe her? Come on, mum, do you?'

'I . . . ' his mother began, and then she was interrupted by a familiar lisping voice.

'You *do* believe me, mummy, don't you?'

Julie was standing at the kitchen door. Edward wondered how long she'd been there. And how much she'd heard.

'Of course I do, darling,' Mrs Bennett said quickly. 'Now run along, both of you. Or I'll never have tea ready in time.'

Julie stared at Edward for a moment with her cold blue eyes, and then she went out of the kitchen as quietly as she'd entered it.

Tea passed off smoothly enough. Julie seemed to be on her best behaviour, but that was probably because her friends were there and she wanted to create a good impression. Edward followed her example. Julie didn't look at him or speak to him, but there was nothing unusual about that. She and the others chattered brightly about nothing in particular, and Edward said nothing at all.

It was dusk by the time they'd finished tea, and it was

then that Julie suggested that they all play ghosts. She looked straight at Edward when she said this, and the proposal seemed like a challenge.

'Can anyone play?' he asked. 'Or is it just a game for horrible little girls?'

'Edward!' warned his mother.

'Of course you can play, Edward,' said Julie. 'You *must* play.'

'But not in the kitchen or the dining room,' said Mrs Bennett. 'And keep out of our bedroom. I'll go and draw all the curtains and make sure the lights are switched off.'

'All right,' said Julie, and the other little girls clapped their hands with excitement.

'How do we play this stupid game?' asked Edward.

'Oh, it's easy,' said Julie. 'One of us is the ghost, and she has to frighten the others. If the ghost catches you and scares you, you have to scream and drop down on the floor. As if you were dead.'

'Like "Murder in the Dark"?' asked Sally.

'Yes,' said Julie. 'Only we don't have a detective or anything like that.'

'It sounds a crummy game to me,' said Edward. 'I don't think I'll play.'

'Oh, *do!*' chorused Sally and Rachel. 'Please!'

And Julie came up to him and whispered, 'You *must* play, Edward. And don't forget what I said this morning; about my ghost, and how it's going to get you with its claws!'

'You must be joking!' Edward jeered. 'And anyway, I told you. Ghosts don't have claws.' He looked her straight in the eyes. 'Of course I'll play.'

Julie smiled, and then turned to the others and said, 'I'll be the ghost to start with. The rest of you run and hide. I'll count up to fifty and then I'll come and haunt you.'

Sally and Rachel galloped upstairs, squealing with excitement. Edward wandered into the hall, and stood for a moment wondering where to hide. It wasn't going to be easy. Their small brick box of a house didn't offer many possibilities. After a while he decided on the sitting-room. It was the most obvious place, and Julie would never think of looking there. He opened the door quietly, ducked down behind an armchair, and waited.

Silence settled over the house. Apart from washing-up sounds from the kitchen, all was quiet. Edward made himself comfortable on the carpet, and waited for the distant screams that would tell him that Sally had been discovered, or Rachel. But no sounds came. As he waited, ears straining against the silence, the room grew darker. The day was fading and it would soon be night.

And then, suddenly, Edward heard a slight noise near the door. His heart leaped and, for some reason, his mouth went dry. And then the fear returned, the unaccountable fear he had felt that morning when Julie hissed her threat through his bedroom door.

The air seemed much colder now, but that could only be his imagination, surely. But he knew that he wasn't imagining the wild thumping of his heart, or the sickening lurching of his stomach. He remembered Julie's words and swallowed hard.

'The ghost'll get you, Edward. With its claws. With its sharp, horrible claws.'

He heard sounds again, closer this time. A scuffle. Whispering. Or was it whispering? Someone was there. Something. He tried to speak, but gave only a curious croak. 'Julie?' he said. 'I know you're there. I know it's you.'

Silence. A dark terrible silence. And then the light snapped on and the room was filled with laughter and shouts of, 'Got you! Caught you! The ghost has caught you!' He saw Julie's face alive with triumph and delight, and, behind her, Sally and Rachel grinning, and the fear was replaced by an anger far darker and more intense than the terror he'd felt before.

'Edward's scared of the ghost!' Julie jeered. 'Edward's a scaredy cat! He's frightened! He's frightened of the gho-ost!'

'I'm not!' Edward shouted. 'I'm not scared! There isn't a ghost!' He pushed past Julie and ran out of the room and up the stairs. He'd show her. He'd prove she didn't have a ghost. There were no such things as ghosts. She didn't have a ghost in her room. She didn't.

Julie's bedroom was empty. Apart from the furniture and the pictures and the toys and dolls and knick-knacks. He opened the wardrobe and pulled shoes and games out on to the floor. He burrowed in drawers, scattering books and stuffed animals and clothes around him. At last he stopped, gasping for breath. And turned.

His mother was standing in the doorway, staring at him in amazement. Clustered behind her were the puzzled, anxious faces of Sally and Rachel. And behind them, Julie, looking at him with her ice-blue eyes.

'What on earth are you doing?' his mother asked.

'See?' he panted. 'There isn't a ghost here. She hasn't got a ghost in her bedroom. There's nothing here. Nothing.'

'Isn't there?' said Julie. 'Are you sure you've looked properly?'

Sally – or was it Rachel? – gave a nervous giggle.

'That's enough,' said Mrs Bennett. 'Now I suggest you tidy up the mess you've made in here, Edward, and then go to your room. I don't know why you're behaving so strangely. But it's got to stop. It's got to.'

She turned and went downstairs. Sally and Rachel followed her. Julie lingered by the door and stared mockingly at Edward. He stared back.

'It's still here, you know,' she said at last. 'The ghost is still here. And it'll get you.'

'You're a dirty little liar!' he shouted. 'A nasty, filthy little liar!'

Julie gaped at him for a moment, taken aback by the force of his rage. Then, 'It'll get you!' she screamed. 'With its claws. Its horrible claws. It'll get you tonight. When you're asleep. Because I hate you. I hate you. Yes, it'll *really* get you. Tonight.'

*

It was dark when Edward awoke. At first he didn't know where he was. And then he remembered. He was in bed. In his bedroom. It was the middle of the night. And he remembered, too, Julie's twisted face and the things she said. The face and the words had kept him awake, and had haunted his dreams when at last he slept.

It was ridiculous, really. All this fuss about an imaginary ghost. Why did he get in such a state over Julie? She was only a little kid after all. His baby sister. You were supposed to love your sister – not fear her. But no, he wasn't *really* afraid of her. How could he be? Such a sweet little girl with blue eyes and fair bouncing curls who was half his age. A little girl who

played games and imagined things. Who imagined ghosts. A ghost in her bedroom.

But he *was* frightened. He knew that now. And as his fear mounted again, the room seemed to get colder. He shut his eyes and snuggled down under the blankets, shutting out the room and the cold. But not the fear.

And then he heard it. A sound. A faint, scraping sound, as though something heavy was being dragged along the landing. A sound that came closer and grew louder. A wet, slithering sound. And with it came a smell, a sickening smell of drains and dead leaves and decay. And the sound grew louder and he could hear breathing, harsh breathing, long choking breaths coming closer.

'Julie?' Edward said, and then he repeated it louder. 'Julie!'

But there was no answer. All he heard was the scraping, dragging sound coming closer, closer. Near his door now. Closer.

'I know it's you!' Edward shouted, and he heard the fear in his own voice. 'You're playing ghosts again, aren't you? Aren't you?'

And then there was silence. No sound at all. Edward sat up in bed and listened. The awful slithering noise had stopped. It had gone. The ghost had gone.

He hugged himself with relief. It had been a dream, that's all. He'd imagined it. Just as Julie imagined things. Imagined ghosts.

Then he heard the breathing again. The shuddering, choking breaths. And he knew that the thing hadn't gone. That it was still there. Outside his door. Waiting. Waiting.

And Edward screamed, 'Julie! Stop it! Stop it! Please stop it! I believe you! I believe in the ghost!'

The door opened. The shuddering breaths seemed to fill the room, and the smell, and the slithering wet sound of a shape. Something was coming towards him, something huge and dark and . . .

He screamed as the claws, yes, the claws tore at his hands, his chest, his face. And he screamed again as the darkness folded over him.

*

When Julie woke up and came downstairs the ambulance had gone. Her mother was sitting alone in the kitchen, looking pale and frightened. She smiled weakly when she saw Julie, and then frowned.

'Darling,' she said. 'I did so hope you wouldn't wake up. I didn't want you to be frightened . . .'

'What's the matter, mummy?' asked Julie. 'Why are you crying?'

Her mother smiled again, and drew Julie to her, folding her arms around her so that she was warm and safe. 'You must be very brave, darling,' she said. 'Poor Edward has been hurt. We don't know what happened but he's been very badly hurt.'

'Hurt? What do you mean, mummy?'

Her mother brushed a stray curl from the little girl's face. 'We don't know what happened, exactly. Something attacked him. His face . . . ' Her voice broke then, and she looked away quickly. 'He has been very badly scratched. They're not sure if his eyes . . . ' She stopped and fumbled in her dressing-gown pocket for a tissue.

'I expect my ghost did it,' Julie said smugly.

'What did you say, dear?'

Julie looked up at her mother. 'My ghost did it. I told

it to. I told it to hurt Edward because I hate him. The ghost hurt him. The ghost in my bedroom.'

Mrs Bennett stared at Julie. 'This is no time for games,' she said. 'We're very upset. Your father's gone to the hospital with Edward. We don't know if . . . ' Her eyes filled with tears. 'I'm in no mood for your silly stories about ghosts, Julie. Not now. I'm too upset.'

'But it's true,' Julie said. 'My ghost *did* do it. Because I told it to.'

Mrs Bennett pushed her away and stood up. 'All right, Julie, that's enough. Back to bed now. You can play your games tomorrow.'

'But it's not a game,' Julie persisted. 'It's true! My ghost . . . '

And then she saw the angry expression on her mother's face, and she stopped. Instead, she snuggled up to her and whispered, 'I'm sorry, mummy. You're right. I *was* pretending. I was only pretending about the ghost. There isn't a ghost in my room. I was making it all up. And I'm so sorry about poor Edward.'

Mrs Bennett relaxed and smiled and drew Julie to her once again. 'That's my baby,' she said softly. 'That's my sweet little girl. Of course you were only pretending. Of course there wasn't a ghost. Would I let a nasty ghost come and frighten my little girl? Would I? Would I?'

'No, mummy,' said Julie. 'Of course you wouldn't.'

'Off you go to bed now.'

'Good night, mummy,' said Julie.

'Sleep well, my pet,' said her mother.

And Julie walked out of the kitchen and into the hall and up the stairs to her bedroom. She went inside, and closed the door behind her.

And the ghost came out to meet her.

'She doesn't believe me, either,' Julie said. 'We'll have to show her, won't we? Just as we showed Edward.'

And the ghost smiled, and nodded. And they sat down together, Julie and the ghost, and decided what they would do.

Mother's Little Helper

I could tell that something was wrong the minute I arrived home and discovered my grandmother sitting in the kitchen. I don't like my grandmother much. People always look very shocked when I tell them this, but I can't see why. Grandmothers are people just like everyone else. Some of them are nice and some of them aren't. I just happen to have been landed with one of the duds, that's all.

Anyway, there she was, squatting in the kitchen like a purple crow. Purple because of the colour of her trouser-suit, and crow because of her beak-like nose and her black hair. My sister Claudia always says that grandmothers shouldn't look like that; they're supposed to have white hair and mittens, and they're supposed to regard their dear grandchildren tenderly through tiny spectacles as they busy themselves with their knitting. They are also supposed to give their grandchildren presents, and take them to zoos and pantomimes.

Our grandmother couldn't be more different. We hardly ever see her, for one thing, mainly because she lives in Bedfordshire, but also because she doesn't like my father. She thinks that my mother, her only daughter, could have done a good deal better for herself. My mother should have married a rich businessman, instead of a penniless music teacher, and she shouldn't have had so many children. (There are seven of us, so far, which may explain why my father is penniless.) When my grandmother *does* come and see us, she doesn't take us out to zoos and pantomimes but spends her time complaining that there isn't a washing-machine, or an electric can-opener, or a microwave oven in our house. And she gives us orders instead of presents. But, as my mother keeps telling us, we really shouldn't complain: she *is* the only grandmother we've got.

Even so, I wasn't overjoyed to find her sitting in our kitchen that afternoon.

'Ah, Olivia,' she said when she saw me, and gave me a very thin smile.

I went over to kiss her. I hate kissing people at the best of times, but I hate kissing my grandmother most of all. Her skin feels like brown paper that's been used over and over again.

'This is a sorry state of affairs,' she said, when the ordeal was over.

I knew she wasn't talking about my kissing her, though it would have been a pretty good description.

'Your poor mother,' she went on. 'I do hope that she'll see sense when all this is over.'

And then I realized what had happened. My mother had gone into hospital to have the latest baby. This explained why my grandmother was skulking in our kitchen; she had come to look after us. My heart sank. I was so used to my mother looking like a block of flats that I'd quite forgotten that a baby was the cause of her extraordinary bulk.

'You got here very quickly,' I said ungraciously. 'And really, you shouldn't have bothered. We can quite easily cope on our own.'

Grandmother scowled, and then looked round the kitchen in search of evidence that we couldn't manage without her. She looked in vain, of course. The kitchen was immaculate, thanks to Mother's Little Helper.

'My case was packed and waiting,' grandmother said. 'I drove down as soon as your father phoned.'

I realized then how quiet the house was. 'Where *is* dad?' I asked quickly.

'With your mother, of course,' grandmother said disapprovingly. 'I shall stay with you until she gets back, and for a few days after that, I expect. But then,' she threatened, 'other arrangements will have to be made.'

'What do you mean?' I didn't like the sound of this.

'Well, your poor mother can hardly manage this house and all of you, and a husband, *and* a new baby, can she?' my grandmother said, and then added darkly, 'Not to mention everything else.'

'We can help,' I said sullenly. 'We always do.'

'Yes, I know that you're a great help to your mother, dear, but I don't think that that will be quite enough. No, someone will have to come in.'

'What sort of someone?' I asked suspiciously.

Grandmother waved a vague hand. 'Oh, a mother's help, or an *au pair,* or somebody,' she said. 'Somebody *useful.*'

That was the last thing we wanted. Or needed. 'We can't afford it,' I said quickly. 'And there's no room.'

'Don't be silly,' my grandmother said severely. 'There's plenty of room. This house is enormous, even for a family the size of yours. And as for cost, well, your father will just have to take in more pupils and stop writing those silly sonatas that no one ever wants to play. Anyway, it shouldn't cost all that much. Not if you find some sort of foreigner.'

'We don't need anyone,' I said. 'We can manage perfectly well on our own. We always have before.'

Grandmother took no notice. She got up from her chair and began to walk restlessly round the room. '*I* can't stay longer than a day or two,' she said. 'There's my heart to think of. And Charlotte. I can't leave her for longer than a week.'

I snorted. Charlotte was a very fat cocker spaniel who looked and smelt like an elderly compost heap. Still, even though she was possibly the most unpleasant dog in the world, we all had every reason to be grateful to her. If it wasn't for Charlotte, my grandmother might visit us more often and stay longer when she did. So, 'No, you mustn't leave Charlotte,' I said, and meant every word.

'Someone will have to come in,' my grandmother decided. She ran a finger along a window-sill in search of dust. And didn't find any. 'I don't know how your mother manages as it is. I really don't.'

Most people don't know how mother manages. Our house is a very large Victorian rectory, with echoing high-ceilinged living-rooms and two floors of bedrooms. And there are attics, and outhouses, and sheds to be looked after as well.

'How on *earth* do you keep it so clean?' people say to my mother. 'It must take every minute of every day. Or an army of charladies.' And mother laughs gaily, and mutters something about having Reliable Help before quickly changing the subject.

But, as people are always quick to point out, there isn't just the house to be considered. There are all the children (seven of us, as I've said). *We* have to be fed, watered, clothed, educated and amused. Not to mention two Labradors, a Cairn Terrier, a budgerigar, a goat, six indeterminate and indistinguishable cats, and a shifting population of rabbits, gerbils, hamsters and guinea-pigs. And there are always extra people staying in the house: odd cousins from Scotland or Australia, and Aunt Evadne whenever she grows tired of Eastbourne, and strange bearded people that my mother meets at political demonstrations. We gave space to a family of Vietnamese boat people for a month, and East African Asian refugees before that. And only the other week we looked after an entire Polish string quintet who were friends of someone who'd known my father when he was a student at the Royal College of Music. It isn't just a question of finding time to look after the house and its occupants, as my mother's friends never tire of reminding her. Every minute of her day seems to be consumed by one or other of her interests: committees for the relief of Oriental famine and South American poverty; campaigns to save whales, rural England and the parish church roof; demonstrations against battery farming, nuclear weapons, and whichever government is in power; meetings of the District Council, the local branch of the RSPCA, and the Women's Institute. And that isn't all. She also finds time to deliver meals on wheels, learn how to play the clarinet, write novels which are never published, make costumes for the amateur operatic society, and study for an Open University degree in History. And when people ask her how she manages, all she does is shrug her shoulders, and laugh, and say that God alone knows. Which isn't quite true. *We* know; the family knows. We all know about Mother's Little Helper.

I can't remember when we first realized that Mother's Little Helper had moved in. It was a long time ago, I know, because my sisters Laura, Julia, and Lydia couldn't remember a time when Mother's Little Helper hadn't been with us. Those of us who *could* remember the time before, were all agreed that the change came shortly after our holiday in Greece. So Mother's Little Helper had been with us for six years at least. But although we were all used to having Mother's Little Helper in the house, none of us had ever seen it and none of us knew who or what it was. All we knew was that Mother's Little Helper could be relied on to take care of all the boring jobs around the house that no one else wanted to do. And we knew (but people outside the family didn't, of course) that Mother's Little Helper was the reason why mother could manage.

It was Mother's Little Helper who made the beds, and did the cleaning and the washing-up. It was Mother's Little Helper who dusted and swept and mopped. It was Mother's Little Helper who saw to the washing and the ironing, who cleaned up after Claudia (who is famous for her untidiness), who made sure that beds were aired for guests, and who cleaned the windows. It didn't seem to venture out of doors much, and ignored father's pleas to mow the lawn and do a little light weeding from time to time. And Mother's Little Helper didn't do any cooking, either, which was a pity, as we were all hopeless at it. Laura thinks that this may be because it is frightened of electricity but I suspect that the real reason is that it just doesn't like cooking.

Mother's Little Helper did have bad days, of course, just like everyone else. Sometimes we had to reprimand it for not washing a knife properly, or for being slapdash with the ironing, but this didn't happen often. And sometimes Mother's Little Helper would be in a bad mood, and the odd plate might suddenly fly across the room and smash against a wall, or angry clanging sounds might come from the kitchen. We didn't take any notice, of course, as we were used to it, but visitors were sometimes taken aback by odd noises in the night, and by the cutlery that occasionally leaped to the floor of its own accord. Most of the time, though, we didn't hear a peep from Mother's Little Helper. And the only evidence we ever had that it was there at all were the gleaming plates drying by the sink, and the piles of freshly laundered sheets in the linen cupboard, and the scent of polish that filled the air when Mother's Little Helper had been at work in the sitting-room.

Grandmother didn't know about Mother's Little Helper, of course. She wouldn't have believed it if we'd told her. But this was why she didn't know how my mother could manage, and this was why we didn't need anyone, foreign or otherwise, to come in and help.

'We can cope,' I repeated. 'We really can.'

Grandmother smiled at me, and patted my shoulder. 'You're a good child, Olivia. But you're at school most of the day. You *all* are except for – what's her name? I do find it so hard to remember who's who.'

'Lydia,' I said.

'Yes, Lydia. And she's too young to help.'

'There's time *after* school,' I pointed out. 'And at weekends. Lavinia's jolly good at cooking. And Claudia and I can do the cleaning . . . '

'It won't be as easy as that,' grandmother said. 'No,' she went on, raising her hand to stop me interrupting again, 'someone will have to come in. I'll discuss it with your parents as soon as I can.'

'But . . . ,' I began, but was interrupted by an ear-splitting crash behind me.

Grandmother gasped, and her eyes widened in alarm.

'What's happened?' I asked, and turned round to look.

'That plate,' my grandmother said, 'that large plate on the dresser. The one with cockerels on it. It – it fell off the shelf. Just like that. All by itself.'

'Oh dear,' I said, and went to pick up the pieces.

'You don't sound very surprised,' my grandmother said in an injured tone. '*I've* never seen anything like it in my life. It's made me feel quite ill.' And she fumbled in her handbag for the bottle of tablets she carried everywhere with her.

'Oh, it happens all the time,' I said airily. 'Probably a slight earth tremor.'

But I knew that we hadn't been alone in the kitchen. And that Mother's Little Helper hadn't liked our conversation one bit.

*

After that, my grandmother didn't bring up the subject again for a day or two. I think that secretly she was just as excited as we were about the new arrivals (the baby had proved to be twins, Augusta and Livia), and she had forgotten about finding help for my mother in all the confusion and celebration that accompanied her return from hospital. In fact, it wasn't until the last evening of her stay that my grandmother mentioned it again.

'Someone will have to come in and help,' she

announced. 'You can't manage on your own, Antonia.'

I had warned my mother in advance, so she was ready with her response. 'I can manage quite well,' she said firmly. 'And anyway, we can't afford it. It's quite out of the question.'

'Ah, but that's where you're wrong,' grandmother said craftily. 'I shall pay the person's wages. I *demand* that you arrange for someone to come and live in. An *au pair* or something. I'm quite prepared to pay. Indeed, I insist upon it.'

We all looked at each other in alarm. None of us had expected this. There was nothing that anyone could say.

'It – it's very kind of you, mother-in-law,' my father said at last. 'But where would we put this person? We've no room.'

'Nonsense.' Grandmother stared at my father as though he were something she had just discovered under a stone. 'There's plenty of room in this barracks of a house. You can get rid of Derek, for a start.'

'Who's Derek?' asked Claudia.

Derek was a student at the local Tech. who lodged in one of the attic rooms. He was so quiet that we hardly knew he was there. Claudia had never seen him at all.

'Derek will stay where he is,' said mother.

'Then it will have to be one of the guest bedrooms,' my grandmother decided.

'And what happens when we have guests?' my father wanted to know.

'They will just have to make do,' said grandmother. 'Or else stay away. I'll make the arrangements as soon as I get home.' And she sailed out of the room in triumph.

We all looked at each other miserably in the silence that followed. I hoped that Mother's Little Helper hadn't overheard what was said but, as there was silence from the kitchen, I assumed that it was safely tucked up for the night.

'Well, that's that,' my father said at last.

'We'll just have to make the best of it,' my mother added cheerfully.

'But will Mother's Little Helper make the best of it?' said Lavinia, who had a practical mind. 'We'll just have to wait and see.'

*

We didn't have to wait very long. As soon as she got back to Biggleswade, my grandmother sprang into action. She telephoned an agency in London which supplied mothers' helps, and a few days after that we were instructed to go to the railway station to meet a person called Giovanna. A few days after *that,* we returned to the railway station to put Giovanna back on the train to Waterloo. Her stay had been a very short one indeed.

It would be easy to lay all the blame on Mother's Little Helper, I suppose. But that wouldn't really be fair. Mind you, Mother's Little Helper didn't help much by turning Giovanna's room upside-down every time she left it (Giovanna blamed Laura for this, which was unkind), and by hiding all her underwear on her first morning with us. But a lot of the blame lay with Giovanna herself. She was fat and Italian with a moustache, and she spent most of the short time she was with us weeping on my mother's shoulder, and making long and noisy telephone calls to her own mamma in Ferrara. Augusta and Livia screamed their heads off every time they saw her, which limited her usefulness as a mother's help, and the crunch came when Derek arrived home late one night and staggered drunkenly into her bedroom by mistake. We had all forgotten to tell Giovanna about Derek, and so she could be forgiven for thinking that she was about to be attacked by a violent intruder. I'll say one thing for Giovanna, though: she was a pretty good screamer. All our neighbours heard her, which is why someone sent for the police.

Grandmother wasn't at all deterred by the sudden departure of Giovanna, even though we tried very hard to persuade her to drop the idea. But she wouldn't listen, which is why we went to the station two days later to welcome Ingrid. She was solemn and Swedish, with long fair hair and a deep voice. She was also very untidy and so she didn't even notice when Mother's Little Helper turned her room upside-down. We made a point of telling her about Derek, but this proved to be a mistake for she fell violently in love with him and spent all the time she was with us drifting around the house saying how unhappy she was. She ignored the babies completely (and one could hardly blame her for they were pretty foul at the best of times), and she didn't attempt to do any housework. After a week we had to ask Ingrid to leave. The only person who was sorry to see her go was my mother, who had hoped for lessons in Conversational Swedish.

It was clear from the moment that we first set eyes on Anneke that she would be harder to shift than the others. She was Dutch and efficient, with a bright smile and broad shoulders. The twins took to her at once, which was a bad sign, and she didn't fall in love with Derek, which showed that she had her wits about her.

She didn't telephone her mother (or anyone else, come to that), and she didn't keep saying how miserable she was. She seemed to enjoy housework, and she endeared herself to my father by announcing her willingness to help in the garden. 'We Dutch people have a great fondness for horticulture,' she informed him. 'Let me see where your grass-mow-machine is.'

Mother's Little Helper had clearly been lulled into a false sense of security by the speed with which Giovanna and Ingrid had come and gone, and so it was a day or two before it woke up to the fact that Anneke would be a harder nut to crack. The first indication we had that Mother's Little Helper had sprung into action came one morning at breakfast when Anneke bounced into the kitchen as usual and said, 'Oh, what larks and japes you are up to.'

We looked at her blankly. Anneke's English wasn't always easy to follow.

'You are pretending you do not understand,' she boomed. 'But I can take a joke, do not worry.'

'What on earth are you talking about?' Claudia said rudely.

'My bedroom,' Anneke said. 'When I went up to my room last night, what a mess was there. My bed was upside-down and my clothes were all topsy-turvy and higgledy-piggledy. Goodness, what larks!'

'*We* didn't do anything,' I said coldly. 'Don't blame us.'

Anneke laughed heartily. She did everything heartily. 'You are pulling my legs,' she said. 'I am not as green as I am cabbage-looking. I was not born yesterday, oh no.' She paused to take a hearty bite of toast and marmalade. 'And then in the night what jolly romps,' she went on. 'Such bangings and crashings and thumps. You are trying to frighten me, yes? But do not worry, I enjoy playing games. That is why I like to work with children.' She finished her toast and looked at us brightly. 'Now then, after breakfast I will clean the kitchen. It looks most grubby to me.'

I flinched then. Surely Mother's Little Helper would fling some crockery in reply. But no. The plates stayed firmly in place on the dresser. Mother's Little Helper was clearly biding its time.

Anneke complained cheerfully about the state of her room every morning that week, and about the strange noises that she heard each night. But she wasn't at all perturbed by them. Indeed, she seemed to enjoy the disturbances. 'You are treating me as one of the family,' she said happily. 'I am included in your jolly games. What fun!'

She refused to believe that we weren't responsible, and saw it all as some kind of friendly initiation ceremony. And she seemed quite disappointed when at last they stopped altogether. Mother's Little Helper had clearly grown as bored with them as the rest of us had. And, although there were one or two isolated instances of flying plates and crashing cups, and milk bottles upsetting themselves in Anneke's lap, and garments disappearing mysteriously from her room, it seemed as though Mother's Little Helper had decided, as we had, that little could be done to dislodge her. In fact, *nothing* seemed to dampen her depressing cheerfulness. Until the day when she decided to tidy up the playroom.

As I've said, our house is a very large one. It may not be modern or in the best of condition (Aunt Evadne from Eastbourne was once hit on the head by a chunk of plaster falling from the sitting-room ceiling), but at least there's plenty of room for everybody. On the ground floor, for instance, there's a sitting-room and a dining-room as well as father's music room and mother's study. And there's also the playroom right at the back. This is a large sunny room which is always untidy, and which is always cluttered with books, and dogs, and games, and the television set, and comics, and jigsaw puzzles. It's the room where Claudia does her dressmaking, and where Lavinia keeps her collections of old bottles and seashells. It's where Laura listens to her records, and where Julia plays complicated games with her horrible little friends. The walls are covered with posters, and Lydia's paintings, and postcards, and souvenirs of our holidays. It's the best room in the house. It's also the room that visitors never see, so it doesn't really matter if it's tidy or not. Even Mother's Little Helper doesn't bother with it much. But Anneke saw it as a challenge, and none of us could be bothered to stop her when she announced one Saturday morning that she was going to tidy it.

It took Anneke all morning. Every so often she would emerge, bedraggled and dusty, to carry boxes of rubbish out to the dustbin. To start with, she asked our opinion before throwing anything away, but we soon grew tired of that and just let her get on with it. We could always rescue important things from the dustbin afterwards.

When lunchtime came, she sat down at the table with a triumphant grin on her face. 'There!' she said, as she piled a generous helping of cottage pie onto her plate. 'The room is now clean and lovely once again. But, my goodness, what a lot of rubbish there was! Newspapers, old comics, books with no covers, toffee papers.' She chuckled to herself. 'Do you know there was an old jam sandwich behind the television? And some potatoes under a chair.'

'I hope you kept the potatoes,' my mother said. 'Waste not, want not.'

'But no,' Anneke said severely. 'These were potatoes with long white shoots growing from them. I did not keep them. And,' she chortled again, 'there was an old shoe. An old black shoe. Of course I threw that away.'

There was a sudden crash, and we all jumped. Two plates had fallen from the dresser and were lying in pieces on the floor.

'My word,' began Anneke. 'How did that – '

There was another crash, as more plates fell. And then, Anneke's plate of cottage pie suddenly rose into the air, hovered above her head for a moment, and turned over. Anneke screamed as her generous helping of meat, carrot and potato streamed down her face and hair and trickled slowly into her lap.

I didn't know whether to laugh or cry, and neither did the others. We stared at Anneke in astonishment. Then we all scampered for the door as an unseen hand swept across the table, pushing plates, and knives, and sauce bottles, and a stone jar of wild flowers onto the floor in a confused mass of broken china, water and cottage pie. The noise silenced Anneke at last. She jumped up and followed us from the room.

We looked at her curiously. Perhaps Mother's Little Helper had done the trick at last. Perhaps Anneke would go and leave us in peace.

'Golly!' Anneke panted. 'Your English practical jokes are very clever.' She brushed a dollop of mashed potato from her nose and said, 'Now I must go and wash, and change, and shampoo my hair. Then it is time to cut the hedges.' She headed for the stairs and then turned. 'I will not clean the mess in the kitchen. You played the joke, so *you* clean it up.' And she marched defiantly up the stairs.

'*Well!*' Claudia said when Anneke had gone. 'Your Little Helper certainly made its mark *that* time, mother dear!'

'Yes,' my mother said. 'But I do wish that it wouldn't break such a lot of plates. They're so expensive to replace. Why doesn't it throw things that bounce?'

Claudia and I went back into the kitchen to inspect the damage.

'What a mess,' I said. 'I wonder why Mother's Little Helper was so angry?'

'Yes, it *was* odd.' Claudia burrowed under the sink for a dustpan and brush.

'It was awfully cross. Do you think it was something Anneke said?'

Claudia crouched down and began to brush fragments of plate into the dustpan. 'Could be,' she said. 'What was she talking about just before it happened?'

I tried hard to remember. 'I think she was telling us about the things she'd found in the playroom. A jam sandwich, I think, and potatoes . . . '

'And a shoe,' said Claudia.

'Yes, that's right. I wonder whose shoe it was? Not one of mine.'

'Nor mine.' There was a clatter as Claudia emptied the dustpan into the bin.

Then, 'I know,' I said excitedly. 'Perhaps it was that funny old shoe we found in Greece. In that village.'

'Yes, it *must* be,' said Claudia. 'I remember it now.'

When we were on holiday in Greece six years ago, Lavinia had found an old shoe lying in the dust at the side of a road. It was black and twisted by age and heat and sunlight, and the buckle was rusted. It was tiny, and had probably belonged to a child or an old woman. We had brought it home along with the other more glamorous souvenirs of our holiday, and it must have been lying in a corner of the playroom ever since.

'It doesn't make sense, though, does it?' said Claudia.

'No, it doesn't,' I said slowly. 'It makes no sense at all.'

Strange things continued to happen for the rest of the day. It was almost as though Mother's Little Helper was nursing a grudge, and didn't want us to forget it. Anneke fell headlong into some rose bushes and insisted that someone had pushed her, although there was no one anywhere near. At tea-time, the table suddenly tipped up, and all the cups and saucers slid onto the floor. And every time the twins stopped yelling and fell asleep, someone, or something, woke them up again. By the time darkness fell, tempers were becoming frayed and, when the lights started to switch themselves on and off, even Anneke's patience began to wear dangerously thin.

'I do not like what is happening,' she said. 'A joke is a joke, but you are going too far. Please stop it. I want you to stop now.' And her lower lip trembled ominously.

'But it's *not* a joke,' my mother said. 'We're not responsible for what's been happening.'

'Then who is?' Anneke demanded. 'Who is responsible? Perhaps the house is haunted. Is that what you are saying?' When no one replied, she snapped, 'Oh, you English are so *stupid!* I am going to my bedroom. Goodnight.' And she stalked angrily upstairs for the second time that day.

We all went to bed early that night, not because we were tired but because Mother's Little Helper continued to play havoc with the lights downstairs. After that everything was quiet until, suddenly, I leaped awake at the sound of a scream, and then another, and another.

I didn't know what time it was, but it must have been the middle of the night because it was pitch dark outside. The screams had woken everyone else, too, judging by the noise of opening doors and wailing babies that filled the air.

I jumped out of bed and opened my bedroom door. The screams were coming from Anneke's room. I crept along the passage towards it, and then yelped with fright as I collided with someone standing outside her door.

'It's only me,' Claudia said, and 'I'm here, too,' came from Lavinia.

'What's going on?' I asked.

'Dunno. Sounds as though she's being murdered.'

'Why don't you go in and see what's happening?' I suggested.

'*You* go in,' Claudia said.

'No, *you.*'

'I think it'd be best to wait for dad,' said Lavinia at last. 'Just in case.'

My father came padding down the corridor, followed by Laura. 'What's all the noise about?' he grumbled.

'It's Anneke,' I explained. 'But we don't know what's wrong.'

'Well then, it's about time we found out,' he said, and turned the handle and pushed.

The door swung open and the screams grew even

louder. My father switched on the light, and we gasped when we saw the room. It was a mess. Chairs were overturned, clothes were strewn across the floor, and sheets and blankets had been dragged from the bed. The dressing table drawers had been pulled out, and their contents scattered round the room. The place looked as though it had been ransacked by vandals.

Anneke was crouched in a corner of the room, her arms covering her head. She stopped screaming when the light came on, and started to cry instead. Lavinia ran across and put her arms round her, and Claudia and I followed.

'What's the matter, Anneke?' Lavinia asked gently. 'It's all right. There's nothing to be afraid of.'

Anneke looked at her with wild, frightened eyes, and gabbled something in what must have been Dutch. 'There was someone in my room' she said at last. 'Someone doing this damage. Someone throwing my things. I saw her. I saw her.'

Claudia and I looked at Anneke in astonishment, and then at each other. 'You saw *her,* did you say?' Lavinia asked urgently.

Anneke began to sob. 'Yes, I saw her,' she gulped. 'She was so ... so awful. So old and ugly and ... and ...' She began to cry loudly once again.

My mother came into the room, pushed past us, and put her arms round Anneke and led her out. 'Off to bed, you lot,' she said to us as she passed. 'The fun's over.'

I didn't move at first, and neither did the others. Claudia looked at me, her eyes wide with excitement. 'Did you hear what she said?'

'Yes,' I answered. 'And you know what it means, don't you?'

'Yes,' Claudia breathed. 'Anneke has seen Mother's Little Helper.'

*

Anneke caught the first train to London the next morning. We all went to the station to see her off, but it wasn't a very cheerful occasion. Anneke's eyes were red from weeping, and she didn't look at us or say very much. Just as the train was drawing into the station, she turned to my mother and said, 'Thank you for having me. I wish I could have enjoyed myself. But you were unkind with your jokes!' Then she turned to us. 'Which of you dressed up as the woman? Which of you was it? You can tell me now that I am going. Was it you, Olivia?'

I shook my head. 'It was none of us. Believe me, it was none of us.'

'Then it was a ghost, after all?' She gazed at me steadily with her clear blue eyes, and I looked away.

We were all very quiet on the way home in the car.

'I wonder who we'll get next?' Lavinia sighed at last. 'I think Anneke was the best so far.'

'No one,' my mother said firmly. 'I'm going to do what I should have done from the very beginning. I'm going to tell your grandmother that we won't have anyone else. I'm going to tell her that we don't need her money or her help. I'm going to tell her that we can manage on our own.'

No one mentioned Mother's Little Helper. But I expect they were thinking about it. I know that I was. I was thinking long and hard about Mother's Little Helper.

When we got home, I didn't follow the others into the house. Instead, I walked round to the back, to the place where the dustbin was kept. I lifted the lid and burrowed inside. It didn't take me long to find what I wanted. It was just as I remembered it: tiny and black and twisted by age and sunlight. The shoe. The shoe we had found on that dusty road in Greece so long ago.

I carried it carefully into the house and then paused in the hallway. Where should it go now? Somewhere safer than before. Then I remembered the glass cabinet in the sitting room in which my mother kept Coronation mugs, and little vases, and old photographs in silver frames. That was where the shoe belonged.

The cabinet was unlocked, so I opened the door and made a space for the shoe between a photograph of my great-grandfather and a little bust of Queen Victoria. Then I closed the door gently and turned round.

There, standing behind me in the sitting-room, was a little old woman. She was dressed entirely in black, in a shapeless black dress, a baggy black cardigan, and wrinkled black stockings. She wore a black scarf over her head and on her feet were . . . the old woman was wearing only one shoe, a tiny black shoe with a buckle. She had no shoe at all on the other foot. No shoe at all.

The old woman looked at me with bright black eyes that gleamed like marbles in her brown, nut-wrinkled face. Her mouth cracked open in a slow gaping smile. And she winked at me. Then slowly, as I watched, she faded like smoke into the silence of the room.

And I went into the kitchen to join the others.

Silver and Son

At the time when Simon Spooner first started work at Silver and Son, Quality Grocers, the shop had been famous throughout the county and beyond for as long as anyone could remember – and for a great deal longer than that. It was famous not just for the quality of its grocery – though there was none finer for eighty kilometres around – but for the standard of its service to customers, for the cleanliness of the premises, and for the courtesy and efficiency of the staff. It is true that it often took some time to be served, and that queues sometimes stretched well past Boots the Chemists next door but then, where else could one find such fine pepper-cheese bread, or pomegranates, or marrow-flower soup from Mexico? Where else such a range of cheeses and pasta, such exotic spices, such fresh peach-raisin tarts and pumpkin pies? No, it was generally agreed that Silver's was unique and that to shop there was an experience to treasure, however long it might take.

But, as Simon's mother was the first to acknowledge, shopping at Silver's *did* take time. It wasn't too bad if all one wanted was a loaf of herb-and-onion bread, or a couple of pounds of sweet potatoes, or a tin of Chinese pickled vegetables – there was only one queue to join then. But if one wanted all three, together with a Russian vegetable pie, 500 grammes of Roquefort

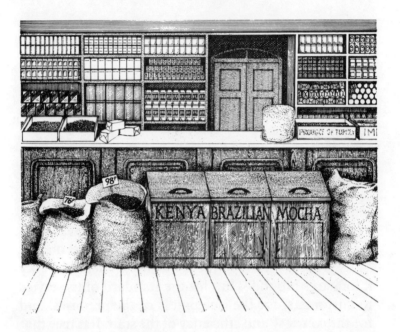

cheese, and some slices of *Schinkenrotwurst,* then half the morning might be spent waiting to be served. For Silver's was an old-fashioned shop which gave old-fashioned service.

To the left as customers entered was the counter for bread, not just ordinary brown or white bread but wholewheat and oatmeal, honey-wheatberry bread and pumpernickel, Irish soda-bread and Swedish rye. One could buy cakes and fruit tarts here, too, as well as chocolate apple strudel and Danish pastries and *profiteroles* bulging with cream. Next to this was the counter for cooked meats and pies, for Toulouse sausages and black puddings and spiced cold pork, for veal-and-partridge pie and frankfurters, for Spanish *chorizos* and *mortadella* from Italy.

Facing that was a counter laden with cheeses: pear-sized Burrini and round red Edam, Cheshire, Cheddar and Leicester, Parmesan and Bel Paese, Gorgonzola and Derby Sage. And then, nearest the door, piles of vegetables from all over the world: bean sprouts and water chestnuts, samphire and sea kale, cardoons, celeriac and kohlrabi. And fruit, too: pawpaws and guavas and grenadillas, cranberries and quinces, smooth nectarines and fresh ripe figs.

Beyond the first room was another, and this was to become Simon's favourite. For here were displayed tins and jars of foreign food with fascinating names that Simon could only pretend to pronounce. Here were to be found exotic soups like *okrochka* from Greece and *kalakeitto* from Finland, Russian *borsch* and Spanish *gaspacho,* Danish buttermilk and New England clam chowder. There were jars with contents that Simon could only guess at: *dolmades* and *golubski, rollmops* and *moussaká, chatchouka* and *melokhia.* And, because this was also the room where the herbs and spices were stored, the air was heady with the savour of rosemary, oregano and fenugreek, of cinnamon, paprika and dill, of the seeds of mustard, fennel and coriander.

Then, laden with their provisions and dazed by the sight and smell of so much gastronomic splendour, Silver's satisfied customers would stagger to an imposing oak kiosk near the door, where Miss Muriel Finch, fierce in high-buttoned blouse and steel-rimmed spectacles, would receive payment for their purchases.

Yes, Silver and Son, Quality Grocers, was a unique establishment. And this was why Simon Spooner was so pleased when he, alone of all the boys in his school, was given a Saturday job there. Saturday was the busiest day of the week at Silver and Son, so there was a lot for Simon to do: restocking the shelves when supplies of Swedish pickled herrings or French frogs' legs ran low; carrying freshly made pizzas and salads from the kitchen at the back of the shop to the cooked foods counter at the front; packing customers' purchases into big cardboard boxes ready for delivery; and helping to clean the shop at the end of the day. But these tasks were never arduous, for Silver and Son was a pleasant place, and so were the people who worked there. Even Miss Muriel Finch was not as forbidding as she looked, despite the fact that it was rumoured in the town that a gang of football hooligans had once been reduced to trembling silence by one of her glares.

As Saturday followed Saturday, Simon came to know the staff of Silver and Son very well, just as they came to know him. There were eight assistants altogether, not counting Mr Silver himself or old Mrs Grimmett, who spent all her time in the kitchen at the back, preparing the onion tarts, spiced rice salad, and sweet oatmeal-raisin bread for which the shop was famous. It was Mr Silver, though, who kept an eye on Simon, gave him his orders, and showed him how the shop worked. It was Mr Silver who taught Simon the difference between Danish Blue cheese and Blue Cheshire cheese, who told him what *sauerkraut* was, and who gave him some pickled ox tongue to take home to his mother. It was Mr Silver who showed him the different kinds of pasta and how to distinguish star-shaped *stellette* from *farfalle,* which looked like little bow-ties. And it was Mr Silver who showed Simon how to make celery-and-apple salad, who taught him the difference between globe artichokes, Chinese artichokes, and Jerusalem artichokes, and who gave him French snails to taste for the very first time. And the last.

Which is why Simon was so very surprised and upset when, three months after he had started work at the shop, he heard that Mr Silver had died. Simon had arrived for work as usual one fine summer Saturday morning to find the staff, not at their accustomed posts behind the counters, but gathered in an anxious group in the centre of the shop. When Miss Muriel Finch saw Simon, she took him to one side and gave him the sad news.

'It was very sudden,' she said. 'A heart attack.' She raised a small lace-edged handkerchief to her nose, and sniffed. 'Of course he was getting on in years,' she added. 'Almost eighty, I believe. But all the same, it has come as a shock. A very great shock.'

'What'll happen now?' Simon asked. 'Will the shop close down?'

The suggestion clearly offended Miss Muriel Finch. 'Of course not,' she said firmly. 'What an extraordinary idea! Mr Silver would not want *that*. No, business will continue as usual. Until,' she added mysteriously, 'we hear to the contrary.'

'What d'you mean?' Simon asked.

'Well,' said Miss Finch. 'Mr Silver Junior may have other plans.'

This was the first time that anyone had mentioned Mr Silver Junior, even though he was the Son of Silver and Son. Now that old Mr Silver was dead, however, all the staff were talking about him. It seemed that Mr Silver Junior had been a great disappointment to his father, preferring to work in London rather than earn his living in his father's shop. Simon tried to find out from the others exactly what it was that Mr Silver Junior *did* in London, but no one seemed to know. Herbert Cuff, who looked after the cheese counter, had heard that he owned a night-club in Mayfair, while Mrs Hoffman of Cooked Meats and Pies was convinced that he sold second-hand cars near Shepherd's Bush. Young Millie Bond, who helped in the kitchen, felt sure that Mr Silver Junior was somebody important in television, but she was shouted down.

'Well, we'll soon get a chance to find out for ourselves,' Miss Muriel Finch announced when the door closed behind the last customer that evening. 'I've just been speaking to Mr Silver Junior on the telephone. He's coming home tomorrow for the funeral. And,' she added triumphantly, 'he will be staying to carry on the business.'

And even she had to smile when she heard the loud cheers that rang through Silver and Son then.

The cheering didn't last long. When Simon arrived at the shop the following Saturday, he found the staff of Silver and Son in a very different state of mind. Even Ted Mounter, the life and soul of Vegetables and Fruit, was unusually quiet.

'What a week it's been,' he said to Simon over tea in the tiny staff room behind the kitchen. 'First old Mr Silver going, and now young Mr Silver coming. Talk about a new broom.'

Simon didn't understand, and said so.

'Mr Silver Junior isn't happy with the business,' Ted explained gloomily. 'We don't sell enough of anything and we take too long to sell it. Not cost effective, he says. Turnover not high enough, he says. Profit not high enough, he says.' Ted sipped his tea noisily, and stared sadly into space.

'So what's going to happen?' Simon asked urgently. 'Is he closing the business?'

'Well,' said Ted, 'he's not exactly closing it down.

And he's not exactly keeping it open. But you'll hear for yourself soon enough. There's a meeting of all the staff when the shop closes this evening. And that includes you.'

For the first time since he started work at Silver and Son, Simon couldn't wait for the day to end. At times it seemed as though it never would, and that the long queues of customers at each counter would never cease, and that the bell in Miss Muriel Finch's cash register would never stop pinging. But, eventually, Miss Finch's bell rang for the last time and the final customer closed the door of the shop behind him. And it was then that the staff gathered slowly in ones and twos, whispering apprehensively to one another. By the time Mr Silver Junior bustled into the shop on the dot of six o'clock, they were all very nervous indeed.

'Well,' Mr Silver Junior said, 'I expect you all know why I want to see you.' He was a smartly dressed middle-aged man, who looked as though he had been a great success at whatever it was he had been doing in London.

'I've been looking carefully at the business during this past week,' Mr Silver Junior went on. 'I've been looking at the figures and seeing what's what. And really, we can't go on as we are. Profits aren't high enough. It's no use selling the best yams in the country if not enough people buy them. There's no point in stocking twenty different kinds of cheese if you only sell ten of them. It isn't good business to keep tins of stuffed vine leaves if you only sell one a month.'

'But we have a reputation to . . . ' began Miss Muriel Finch.

'I know, I know,' he said. 'No one knows that better than I do, dear lady, believe me. But our reputation won't pay the bills. Or your wages. So I'm going to make a few changes.' Mr Silver Junior paused, but if he expected loud protests, he was disappointed. The staff were staring at him poker-faced. 'I'm going to redesign the shop in keeping with current retail practice. We'll be going self-service, for a start. And the stock will cater for the needs of a wider public than it does at present. We'll appeal to all tastes and pockets. But don't worry, all of you – even young Simon there – will have jobs in the new business. With improved pay and conditions. You won't lose out at all. All we'll be doing is taking Silver and Son into the twentieth century and . . .'

'In other words,' interrupted Miss Muriel Finch, 'you'll be changing the shop into a supermarket.'

'Exactly,' smiled Mr Silver Junior. 'Now, are there any questions?'

There were no questions, so Mr Silver Junior bustled out as busily as he'd arrived, leaving behind him a bewildered and silent staff.

'Well!' said Miss Muriel Finch at last. 'If old Mr Silver knew about this, he'd turn in his grave.'

And she turned and stalked grandly out of the shop.

*

During the weeks that followed, Silver and Son, Quality Grocers, changed out of all recognition. To start with, the shop closed down entirely. Then Mr Silver Junior stripped the building of the marble-topped counters, and the wooden shelves which stretched from floor to ceiling, and Miss Muriel Finch's oak kiosk. He removed the old-fashioned windows and decorative tiling at the front, and replaced them with plate glass and steel. He knocked down the wall at the back, and built a new extension which made the shop twice as big as it had been before, and then filled the entire space with gleaming shelves and humming freezer cabinets. He installed doors which opened automatically, air conditioning, fluorescent lighting, and a loudspeaker system. And then, when the building itself was complete, he filled the shelves and freezers with tins and packets and boxes, with baked beans, and dog food and custard powder, with dustbin liners, and dishcloths and rubber gloves, with fish fingers, hamburgers and crispy pancakes. And finally, when the shop was stocked and fitted and ready to open, he put a large neon sign across the front which read: *Silver's Swift-Service Superstore.*

The grand opening of the supermarket was a splendid affair. Reporters and photographers were present to record the event for posterity and, because Mr Silver Junior had arranged for the shop to be declared open by a glamorous television personality called Roxy Trent, crowds of people collected in the street outside to watch. Simon was one of them. Mr Silver Junior began by making a speech about the new supermarket and how it was carrying on a tradition established by his great-grandfather, but something went wrong with the loudspeaker and no one could hear what he said. After that, to the accompaniment of shrill cries of excitement from the crowd, the lovely Roxy Trent cut a ribbon which stretched across the supermarket door and said that she was terribly happy to be there, thank you very much, and that she was pleased to declare Silver's Swift-Service Superstore open. And then Mr Silver Junior invited all present to enter the shop and see for themselves the quality and quantity of the wares on offer.

It was then that the crowd began to disperse. For, as

Simon's mother said, 'When you've seen one supermarket, you've seen them all.' And Simon didn't go
inside either. He was to start work there again the
following Saturday and so he would be able to see it all
for himself then. Anyway, he didn't really want the free
balloon and signed photograph of the lovely Roxy
Trent that Mr Silver Junior was offering to the first
hundred customers.

When Simon arrived at the supermarket the following Saturday, he was astonished at the transformation
that had taken place in the building. Instead of
crowded, friendly rooms piled high with colourful tins
and jars, there was now one long bright space filled
with neatly stacked shelves and freezer cabinets. Instead of the sound of cheerful conversation, all he
could hear was soft sentimental music from the loudspeakers overhead. Instead of the cheerful ping of Miss
Muriel Finch's cash register, there was the monstrous
rattle of the machine at the check-out on which Miss
Finch, scowling heavily and wearing a blue overall
with SSSS on the pocket, added up the contents of
customers' wire baskets. Every now and then, the
loudspeaker music would be interrupted by a gong and
a voice, which sounded suspiciously like the lovely
Roxy Trent, would urge customers not to miss that
week's incredible special offer of two tins of baked
beans for the price of one, or tell them that dog food
was two pence cheaper today. Then the music would
resume, and so would the smooth and efficient running
of the store.

Simon didn't like it at all. And neither did the other
people who had worked at Silver and Son, Quality
Grocers. Ted Mounter was in charge of Vegetables and
Fruit once again, and Herbert Cuff still looked after

Cheese, but they missed the variety of their old jobs. 'All they want is slabs of Cheddar wrapped in plastic,' Herbert complained to Simon, and Ted Mounter added that none of his customers would recognise a melongene if he hit them in the face with one. The only person who had left the shop for good was old Mrs Grimmett, because there was no call for her pimento salad and chicken-and-grouse pie at Silver's Swift-Service Superstore and, as she would be eighty-two years old next birthday, she felt that it was as good a time as any to retire.

Simon's job was more tedious now. Restocking the shelves wasn't much fun when this simply meant piling umpteen cans of soup on top of one another, and he didn't enjoy rescuing the shopping trolleys which customers left in nearby carparks, which was another of his tasks. He missed the warmth and colour of Silver and Son, Quality Grocers; he missed the tang of herbs and spices, the aroma of Mrs Grimmett's freshly-baked corn bread, and the friendly chatter of staff and customers. No one took any notice of him in the supermarket—all the shoppers did was push their trolleys blindly up one aisle and down the next. The only time a customer spoke was to complain about something.

And, oddly enough, there was quite a lot to complain about in those first weeks. One day, it was discovered that all the tins of spaghetti in tomato sauce had been wrongly labelled and contained cat food. On another, a pile of tins of mushroom soup collapsed on top of two elderly ladies. On another, all the freezers suddenly broke down at the same time, with the result that the frozen fish thawed and all the ice cream melted. And on yet another, Miss Muriel Finch's electric cash register went berserk and charged a customer £5263.30 for a packet of peanuts and two pork pies!

Simon was told of these incidents on his second Saturday at work. And it was on his third Saturday that he witnessed strange things himself. He was idly replenishing a shelf of washing-up liquid, and wondering how long it would be until his tea-break, when the syrupy music coming from the loudspeaker stopped, and he heard the familiar ding-dong which signalled the announcement of that day's earth-shattering special offer. But, instead of the familiar lisp of the lovely Roxy Trent, Simon—and everyone else in Silver's Swift-Service Superstore—heard a man's voice say, 'Whatever you do, don't buy any of the bacon in this place. It's disgusting stuff, and if you eat it you'll die of food poisoning.' Then the music started again.

There was a horrified silence in the shop, and then everyone began to talk at once. At first, Simon thought he'd imagined the announcement, but some customers nearby were laughing about it so his ears couldn't have deceived him. And there was something familiar about the voice, too. Simon frowned to himself as he tried to remember where he'd heard it before. Then he was distracted by the sound of running footsteps, and looked up to see Mr Silver Junior running from the front of the shop, where he'd been talking to Miss Muriel Finch about her troublesome cash register, to the office at the back where the loudspeaker system was operated. A moment later the music stopped again, the gong sounded, and this time it was Mr Silver Junior's voice that echoed round the supermarket.

'Ladies and gentlemen,' he said breathlessly, 'please

ignore the previous announcement. All the bacon in this store is of the finest quality, and is stored and served in hygenic conditions that are second to none. Thank you.' The music began again, and Mr Silver Junior emerged from the office looking flustered and puzzled.

Ten minutes later it happened again. The music stopped, and a man's voice announced, 'All the eggs in this shop have gone off. I'd stay well clear of them if I were you.'

Once more there was a horrified silence, and once more Mr Silver Junior galloped into the office where he made an announcement to the effect that the eggs sold in his establishment were fresh and wholesome. This time, though, the customers laughed out loud. But Simon noticed that no one bought any eggs from then on. Or any bacon, come to that.

The announcements continued throughout the day. The mysterious voice advised customers to steer clear of the frozen fish because it was rotten, and then told them that the cheese contained maggots. After that, it caused a stampede by announcing that all tins of spaghetti would be free of charge from then on. It was only when people had kicked and scratched their way to the shelves that the music stopped yet again and the voice added that the tins were only being given away because they were contaminated.

By now a large crowd had collected in the supermarket, not to buy food but to listen to the mysterious voice. Loud cheers greeted each announcement, until the voice got its own back by suddenly shouting, '*Fire!*' It was fortunate that no one was trampled underfoot in the rush for the doors that followed.

This last announcement had finally succeeded where

the others had failed: it cleared the supermarket of customers. Simon and the other assistants returned after a while, when it became apparent that there was no fire, and Mr Silver Junior followed. He locked the door behind them and then turned, his face red with anger.

'Now then,' he said. 'I want an explanation. I want to know what's going on.'

The staff looked at him blankly. 'It's nothing to do with us,' Herbert Cuff said.

'Don't give me that,' sneered Mr Silver Junior. '*I* didn't interfere with the loudspeakers. *I* didn't make those announcements about the eggs and the free tins of spaghetti and . . . '

'What *I* don't understand,' Miss Muriel Finch said sweetly, 'is why you didn't disconnect the loudspeaker system after the first announcement. Then none of this would have happened.'

Mr Silver Junior looked at her and smiled grimly. 'But I did, dear lady,' he said. 'I did switch it off.'

You could have heard a pin drop in the silence that followed.

'Then . . . ' began Ted Mounter.

'Yes,' said Mr Silver Junior. 'Someone's been very clever. Someone's been making a right fool of me. *And* they're putting me out of business into the bargain. And it's not just today. There's been trouble ever since we opened. Things going wrong. The freezers breaking down. And those tins of soup falling on the old ladies.'

Millie Bond giggled nervously, and Mr Silver Junior scowled at her. 'It's nothing to laugh at,' he went on. 'We lost a lot of customers before we even started. It was bad enough last Thursday when all the doors stuck and nobody could get out.'

'And on Monday,' said Herbert Cuff, 'when the music started to play at full blast and we couldn't turn it down.'

'Or off,' added Ted Mounter.

'Don't mention those loudspeakers to me,' growled Mr Silver Junior. 'Now then, which one of you was it? Come on, own up.'

The others looked at each other in silence. And then Miss Muriel Finch said, 'But how could it be one of us? Surely you recognized the voice?'

Mr Silver Junior looked puzzled. 'No,' he said. 'I can't say I did.'

'Well, you ought to have recognized it,' said Miss Finch. 'It was your father's voice. It was old Mr Silver.'

Of course it was, Simon thought. I *knew* the voice was familiar. But how could it be old Mr Silver's voice? Old Mr Silver was dead. It was impossible. Quite impossible. Unless . . .

'What are you trying to tell me?' Mr Silver Junior said. 'Are you trying to say . . . '

'I'm not trying to tell you anything, Mr Silver,' Miss Muriel Finch said calmly. 'All I am saying is that the voice we heard was that of your father. You may draw your own conclusions.' She looked at him steadily through her steel-rimmed spectacles.

Mr Silver Junior met her gaze and then looked nervously away. 'I don't believe it,' he said. 'It can't be.'

Miss Muriel Finch smiled thinly and shrugged her shoulders. Mr Silver Junior looked at her for a moment and then shouted, 'I don't believe it!' He shook his fist at the ceiling, and shouted again, his face purple with rage. 'Leave me alone, you old fool! Leave me alone! *Go away!*'

And then several things happened. All the lights

went out, and the loudspeakers switched on, filling the shop with loud blaring music. On the far side of the room, a pile of tins of macaroni cheese suddenly cascaded noisily onto the floor, and steam began to rise ominously from all the frozen-food cabinets. There was a loud clashing and rattling as a neatly stacked line of shopping trolleys suddenly began to move of its own accord, and headed straight towards Mr Silver Junior.

'No!' he shouted. 'No!' And then, to the ceiling, 'What do you want? What do you want me to do?'

A sudden silence fell as the music stopped playing, the trolleys stopped moving, and the tins of macaroni cheese stopped rolling about on the floor. The steam died down, and the lights came on. And then Miss Muriel Finch's cash register sprang into life. Simon, who was standing right next to it, jumped at the sudden chatter, and watched in amazement as the machine printed out a white paper receipt.

Simon peered at the paper slip and gasped. Where there was usually a long column of figures was now a row of letters. Words. A sentence.

'What – what is it?' Mr Silver Junior asked.

Simon looked at him, his face pale with fright. 'I don't know,' he said. 'The machine's printed words instead of figures. I don't know how . . . '

'But what does it say?' Miss Muriel Finch asked urgently.

Simon looked down at the paper and then up again at the others. They were all staring at him anxiously.

' "Give me my old shop back." ' Simon looked straight at Mr Silver Junior. 'That's what it says: "Give me my old shop back." '

And the slip of paper fell from his fingers and fluttered down to the floor.

*

There was no special ceremony to celebrate the re-opening of Silver and Son, Quality Grocers. The doors opened quietly at nine o'clock on the Monday morning, just as they had always done, and the first customers found to their surprise that the shop looked exactly as it was before old Mr Silver died. Everything was just as it had always been.

To the left, as the shoppers entered, was the counter for bread, for *croissants* and Jewish egg-bread and Norwegian bannocks. Next to that was Mrs Hoffman's Cooked Meats counter, laden with Parma ham and duck *pâté* and Swedish liver sausage, with *pissaladina* and *Kalbfleischwurst* and Polish pork ring. Across the way stood the cheese counter, lovingly tended by Herbert Cuff, and, nearer the door, beaming Ted Mounter looked after the vegetables and fruit, the plantains, pine nuts, and red and green peppers, the breadfruit, mangoes and prickly pears.

Towards the rear of the shop was the section where Simon liked to linger when he came in to work on Saturdays. For here were the packets and tins and jars of food from faraway places: stuffed walnuts from Cyprus, Italian egg noodles, inkfish from Greece, Turkish *burek,* Spanish quince paste, and *taramasalata.* And the herbs and spices were stored here, too: cassia, chillies and cardamom seeds, angelica, saffron and mace.

And then, when they had bought all that they needed, and much that they didn't, the shoppers paused as before to pay for their purchases at the oak kiosk where Miss Muriel Finch sat in splendour. Then Mr Silver Junior opened the door for them, and they walked out into the sunlight, dazed by the sight and smell of so much gastronomic splendour.

Yes, it was generally agreed that Silver and Son, Quality Grocers, was a unique establishment, and that to shop there was an experience to treasure.

Pretty Penny

It was clear to everyone right from the very beginning that little Penny Pearson would go far. Mrs Pearson was convinced of it, and said as much to anyone who would listen. And even the other mothers who watched resentfully from the chairs that lined one wall of The Dottie Denver Academy of Dancing *(Ballet, Tap and Modern Stage Dancing and Singing. Pupils Prepared for All Examinations. Ballroom, Latin American and Disco Dancing Tuition for Adults, By Arrangement)* were inclined to agree with her. Their own children were talented, of course, for had they not been accepted as pupils by Miss Denver, whose standards of excellence were as high as her fees? But little Penny Pearson was more than just talented: she was special. Her pretty face, her fair curls, her cheeky grin, her deft footwork, and her very loud singing all marked her as a child ripe for Discovery. It was said that she could be a new Shirley Temple, or another Petula Clark. It had even been suggested by some that she might turn out to be a second Lena Zavaroni.

But Mrs Pearson and the other mothers were not the only ones who had recognized Penny's star potential. Little Miss Spindle, who played the piano for class and rehearsals, was sure that Penny would have a glittering future. And even Dottie Denver herself, she who had entertained the troops during the war and had met Des

O'Connor, even Dottie Denver could not recall a more
talented pupil. And she was such marvellous publicity
for the Academy as well. An appearance by Penny in
the local amateur production of *The Sound of Music,*
or in Old-Tyme Music Hall at the Princess Beatrice
Eventide Home, was worth ten newspaper advertise-
ments. It was true that Penny had not managed to get
beyond the first stages of the auditions for *Annie* in
London, and that none of the television companies had
expressed an interest in her, despite repeated phone
calls, but then some people just didn't appreciate
genuine talent. Still, there was a good chance that one
or two London agents might attend the Academy's
end-of-term entertainment when it took the stage of St
Winifred's Church Hall in a month's time, and that the
talent of Penny Pearson would then be recognized at
last.

Meanwhile, though, there were problems with the
opening number. Dottie Denver gazed critically at the
line of lumpy little girls in leotards who were pretending to be clouds, and clapped her hands.

'No, *no!*' she shouted. 'You're supposed to be light
and airy and fluffy. At the moment you're more like
dollops of cold porridge.'

The watching mothers bridled. Sometimes Miss
Denver went too far.

'Let's try it once again from the top,' Dottie Denver
called. 'Right, Miss Spindle.'

Little Miss Spindle, huddled at the piano in a grubby
pink cardigan, pounced on the keyboard once again.

'*That's* better,' said Dottie Denver. '*Much* better. On
your *toes,* please, Belinda. That's right. Lovely. Veronica, dear, you really must learn to keep your balance if
you hope to make a career in show business.'

The clouds hopped and shuffled, and then Miss Spindle banged the piano even more loudly, and Penny Pearson, clutching a giant broom, ran in front of the others and posed prettily.

The watching mothers sat up. This should be worth seeing.

Whenever I see those clouds of grey, Penny blared,
Coming to spoil a sunny day,
I go right up to them and say
Go away, clouds! Go away!

She ran along the line of clouds, thumping them viciously with the broom. Each cloud in turn smiled brightly as she passed, and then they all linked arms and began to kick.

'Very nice,' Dottie Denver called out. 'Do keep in time, Veronica dear.'

Whenever I see a rainy sky, Penny bellowed,
Bringing a teardrop to your eye,
I go right up to it and cry
Stay away, rain! Stay away!

'All together now,' said Dottie Denver.

Hullo, May-time! the clouds sang lustily.
Hullo, gay-time!
Hullo, happy day-time!
Brush those clouds away!

The watching mothers smiled at each other. What a clever girl that Penny Pearson was, to be sure. So pretty, too. But—and here they looked furtively at Mrs Pearson—what a pity about the sister.

'Right, that's enough for today,' said Dottie Denver at last. 'This number's coming along quite nicely, but it still needs a *lot* of work. We'll try it again on Saturday morning. Off you go now.'

The clouds broke ranks and ran noisily to the waiting mothers who stood ready with coats and outdoor shoes. Penny Pearson ran to her mother, too, followed more slowly by one of the plumper clouds.

Dottie Denver watched them for a moment and then came to a decision. 'May I see you for a moment, Mrs Pearson?' she called. 'I won't keep you long.' And she sailed towards her office.

Penny Pearson watched her mother follow Miss Denver out of the room and then turned to her sister. 'You do it on purpose, don't you?' she said icily.

'What?' asked Veronica.

'You deliberately fall down and get out of step just to spite me,' said Penny, her eyes like stones in her pretty face.

Veronica met her gaze defiantly. 'You know I don't,' she said. 'You know I do my best. I want to be a good singer. I want to be as good as you.'

Penny laughed. 'You must be joking,' she said viciously. 'You'll never be as good as me. Never.'

She bent down to put on her shoes and so she didn't see the expression on her sister's face. One of the mothers did, though. She turned to her neighbour and said, 'That other Pearson girl's a bad-tempered little thing, isn't she? If looks could kill . . . ' And the two mothers stared and clucked and agreed that it was odd for twin sisters to be so different.

The Pearson sisters were also under discussion in Dottie Denver's office. Mrs Pearson stared at the signed photographs on the wall, and at the framed poster advertising Miss Denver's only London appearance (in the chorus of *Bless the Bride* at the Adelphi in 1947), and wondered whether to shout or cry.

' . . . of course we don't expect the standard of Veronica's work to be as high as Penny's,' Dottie

Denver was saying. 'The trouble is that it is so much worse than *everyone* else's. I'm not going to beat about the bush, Mrs Pearson.' She paused, and wondered whether she was doing the right thing. 'I'm afraid, Mrs Pearson,' she went on, 'that I cannot allow Veronica to appear in the end-of-term show. Her work just isn't good enough. If I may speak bluntly, she would let the side down.'

Mrs Pearson's lower lip trembled. 'Oh dear,' she said. 'Veronica will be awfully upset.'

'I'm afraid that can't be helped,' Dottie Denver said loftily. 'She must learn to cope with disappointment if she is thinking of a stage career. But surely,' and she lowered her voice discreetly, 'surely, Mrs Pearson, you can see for yourself that Veronica isn't quite – quite –' Her mouth opened and shut like a goldfish as she struggled to think of tactful adjectives.

'Well,' said Mrs Pearson, 'I know that she isn't the world's greatest singer . . . '

'It would help if she could keep in tune,' Miss Denver murmured.

' . . . and her dancing is a little ungainly at times . . . '

'*All* the time,' muttered Miss Denver.

' . . . but surely, given patience and encouragement and *your* expert guidance . . . '

You don't get round me *that* way, thought Miss Denver.

' . . . her work will improve,' Mrs Pearson finished.

'But we don't *have* time,' Dottie Denver pointed out. 'The show is only a month away.'

'Ah.' Mrs Pearson paused, and then craftily played her trump card. 'Well, in that case, I'm afraid that you may have to look elsewhere for a leading lady.'

Dottie Denver's jaw dropped.

'Yes, I'm afraid so,' Mrs Pearson went on. 'I'm sure that Penny will refuse to take part in the show if Veronica is removed. They're very close, you see. Being twins. They do everything together.' And she smiled at Dottie Denver in triumph.

Dottie stared back, full of admiration. Very clever, she thought. Very clever indeed. Then she said, 'Well then, perhaps if we keep Veronica in the nursery rhyme number and the lollipop dance . . . '

'And the song from *Oliver!*' put in Mrs Pearson quickly.

'. . . and the song from *Oliver!*' agreed Miss Denver, 'then perhaps she won't object to being left out of the Broadway number at the end.'

Mrs Pearson considered. 'If you insist,' she said at last. 'But it's a great pity. Veronica is so keen. So very keen. She so desperately wants to be a singer and dancer like her sister. She really does.'

Dottie Denver shrugged, and muttered something about silk purses and sow's ears that Mrs Pearson didn't quite catch.

'Well, then,' Mrs Pearson said, standing up. 'I'm glad we understand each other.'

'Yes,' said Dottie Denver. 'So am I.'

'Though how I'm going to tell Veronica, I can't think,' Mrs Pearson said gloomily as she went out.

As it happened, Veronica took the news quite calmly. Mrs Pearson told her in the car on the way home and, apart from assuring her mother that no, honestly, she wasn't at all upset, Veronica didn't say very much. But Mrs Pearson, who was driving, didn't see the smirk of triumph on Penny's face, or the look of hate that Veronica gave her sister in return. And she didn't know that, when they got home, Veronica rushed straight upstairs to her bedroom, locked the door and burst into tears.

Little happened after that to disrupt rehearsals for the end-of-term entertainment. Veronica meekly dropped out altogether from the more vital scenes, and grudgingly consented to occupy obscure positions at the back of the stage in the remaining items. It was from there that she listened to Penny (in a red curly wig) bellowing 'The Sun'll Come Out Tomorrow,' and it was from there that she joined in the chorus as Penny (dressed in decorative rags) brayed 'Consider Yourself at Home,' and it was from there, dressed as a liquorice allsort, that she helped form a background of dancing sweets to accompany Penny's shrill version of 'On the Good Ship Lollipop.'

The watching mothers beamed through all the rehearsals, marvelling at the brilliance and beauty of their daughters. And Dottie Denver smiled and tapped her foot, and hoped that the audience would be so overwhelmed by the talent of Penny Pearson that they wouldn't notice her less favoured sister lurching in the background.

Little Miss Spindle was the only person at the Academy who sympathized with Veronica. 'I think it's a shame, I really do,' she told her during a break in rehearsals for the finale. 'We can't all be talented, can we? They should still give you a chance like everyone else.'

'But I can do it,' Veronica said seriously. 'I *can*. I *will*. I'm going to be as good as her. I'm going to be even better.'

And then Miss Spindle, taken aback by the harsh note in the child's voice and the cold anger mirrored in her eyes, scuttled back to the piano and launched into the opening bars of the closing number.

Veronica watched in silence as Penny strutted across the floor, wearing shorts, fishnet tights and a top hat. Behind her, a row of sullen little girls pretended to be the New York skyline.

I'm just a Broadway baby, Penny shrieked,
Heading for the heights.
Waiting for the crazy day when my name's in lights!

Veronica watched Penny dancing, and Miss Spindle smiling at the piano, and Dottie Denver nodding with approval. And she saw the row of beaming mothers, and her own, blossoming with pride. And she hated them all. Every single one of them. She'd show them. One day she'd show them.

I'll join the stars on the Great White Way, Penny yelled,
And tell 'em this baby's here to stay.
I'm gonna shout hey-hip-hooray!
I'm just a Broadway baby!

'Bravo!' Dottie Denver shouted, as the girls formed the final tableau, and Penny did the splits and waved an American flag energetically. 'That's coming along *very* nicely. Congratulations, Penny dear. That was *super*, really *super*.'

Penny Pearson preened, and everyone broke into spontaneous applause. It was little Miss Spindle, though, who noticed that one person didn't join in. How odd, she thought to herself. How very odd. You'd think she'd be glad to have such a talented sister. You'd think she'd be glad.

*

The accident happened a week later. It was never really clear exactly what took place, because no one else was there at the time. Only Veronica. And she, of course, was much too upset to talk about it. All that the driver could remember was that two little girls had been walking along the pavement towards him and that, suddenly, one of them had fallen into the road in front of his car. He tried to stop, of course, but it was too late. But no one blamed him. It wasn't his fault.

'She lost her balance,' Veronica said when they asked her. 'I think she lost her balance. We were walking along and she started to show me a new dance step, and then – and then she sort of fell. Into the road. And I couldn't stop her. And the car . . . '

It was a tragedy, of course. One of those terrible accidents that happen without any warning. It could have happened to anyone. At any time. But this time it had happened to Penny Pearson.

Dottie Denver and the rest of the Academy staff attended the funeral, and so did most of the mothers. The children were kept away, of course, but Veronica was there, looking pale and anxious in her new black coat. The mothers watched her with sympathetic eyes. The poor lamb. What a dreadful thing to happen. And they were so close, weren't they? Penny and Veronica. Being twins.

Dottie Denver looked at Veronica, and wondered what on earth she was going to do about the end-of-term entertainment. There was no one good enough to take Penny's place. If only it had been the other way round, she thought. If only it had been Veronica and not Penny who had . . . Then she chided herself for harbouring such unkind thoughts, and blew her nose loudly into a little lace handkerchief.

Little Miss Spindle watched Veronica, too, and tried to push from her mind the memory which disturbed her so much, the memory of Veronica looking at her sister with eyes as cold as steel. And Miss Spindle thought of the accident, and wondered.

*

On the Saturday after Penny's funeral, Veronica decided that she would like to resume her classes at The Dottie Denver Academy of Dancing. Her late arrival with her mother not only brought the rehearsal to an embarrassed halt but also succeeded, as nothing else ever had, in stunning Dottie Denver into silence.

Veronica looked round at the curious, awkward faces of the other girls and their mothers, and wondered whether she'd ever get another chance to make such a dramatic entrance.

Little Miss Spindle broke the silence at last, and came rushing up to Veronica and her mother with words of welcome and sympathy. And then Dottie Denver followed.

'It's lovely to see you both,' Dottie said, 'but are you really sure . . . '

'Veronica insisted,' said Mrs Pearson. 'She said the show must go on.'

'It's what Penny would have wanted,' Veronica said simply, and gazed bravely into Dottie Denver's eyes.

'Of course, darling,' Miss Denver said huskily, and turned quickly away so that no one could see her tears.

'You're a real trouper, dear,' Miss Spindle said to Veronica. 'Just take it slowly to begin with.'

Dottie Denver turned back to them, smiling brightly. 'We're just about to do the clouds number,' she said. 'If you like, you could join in the chorus . . . '

'I'd like to sing the song,' Veronica said.

There was a stunned silence. 'Sing the song?' Miss Denver stammered.

'Yes,' said Veronica. 'I'd like to take Penny's part. Just this once. To see if I can do it.'

'But that's ridiculous!' Dottie Denver said. 'You can't even . . . I mean, well, I don't think . . . '

'Perhaps,' interrupted Miss Spindle, 'we might allow Veronica to try. Under the circumstances,' she added pointedly.

'I see what you mean,' said Miss Denver. 'Yes, of course, Veronica. By all means take – take Penny's part this time. We'll see how it goes.'

'You're very kind,' Mrs Pearson murmured, and crossed to join the other mothers on the line of chairs.

There was an awkward silence as Veronica took up her position, and Dottie Denver closed her eyes, fearing the worst. Miss Spindle began to play the opening music, and the clouds skipped and shuffled across the floor. Then she played the notes which were Veronica's cue.

The watching mothers looked away as Veronica ran on with the giant broom. What did the poor child think she was doing?

Whenever I see those clouds of grey, Veronica blared,

Coming to spoil a sunny day,
I go right up to them and say
Go away, clouds! Go away!

She ran along the line of clouds, thumping them viciously with the broom. Each cloud in turn smiled brightly as she passed, and then they all linked arms and began to kick.

'I don't believe it,' Dottie Denver said, opening her eyes. 'I don't believe it.'

Whenever I see a rainy sky, Veronica bellowed,
Bringing a teardrop to your eye,
I go right up to it and cry
Stay away, rain! Stay away!

'It's unbelievable!' Mrs Pearson said, and burst into tears.

Hullo, May-time! the clouds sang raggedly.
Hullo, gay-time!
Hullo, happy day-time!
Brush those clouds away!

The music dwindled into silence. Miss Denver, Miss Spindle and all the girls and their mothers stared at Veronica in astonishment.

'What's the matter?' said Veronica in alarm. 'What's wrong? What have I done?'

No one answered at first. Then Dottie Denver cleared her throat and said, 'Nothing's wrong, dear. It's just — it's just that you — well, I mean — you sound just like Penny. Your voice is exactly the same. And your dancing . . . '

'It's uncanny,' said Mrs Pearson tearfully. 'You're just like her.'

Veronica looked at them wildly. 'I'm not,' she said. 'I'm not like her at all. I'm like me. I'm *me!*'

'I'm sorry, dear,' Miss Denver said firmly. 'You sounded just like Penny. I don't know whether you're doing a clever imitation, or . . . '

'I *didn't* sound like her,' Veronica shouted. 'I'm better than her. I'm better!'

There was an awkward silence. The mothers stared at Veronica in fascinated horror.

'Yes, well, hmnn,' Dottie Denver said at last. 'We'll

see, shall we? Let's try another song. Do you know the words for 'The Sunny Side of the Street'? Good. Miss Spindle, dear, would you oblige? Thank you so much.'

There was no mistaking the voice this time. It was Penny's voice. And only Penny could have tap danced with such exuberance and skill. But it wasn't Penny who was dancing. And Penny wasn't singing. It was Veronica.

Dottie Denver stared at her in amazement. She couldn't believe her eyes or her ears. Suddenly, Veronica could dance. Gone was the stumbling figure who was forever tripping over her own feet. And gone, too, was the tuneless moaning that had marked her attempts to sing. But the footwork was Penny's. And the voice was Penny's. Yet the girl standing there with a defiant, questioning look on her face was Veronica. There was no doubt at all about that.

'Why are you all staring at me?' Veronica said.

'Don't you know?' asked Miss Denver. 'Do you really not know?'

Veronica shook her head defiantly. 'No, I don't,' she said. 'I don't know why you're all looking at me like that. Stop it. *Stop it!*'

Dottie Denver put an arm around her. 'We're surprised, that's all.'

'Surprised that I can sing?' asked Veronica. 'I told you that I could sing. But you wouldn't believe me. You only listened to *her*. You only cared about *her*.'

'But you sound just like my Penny,' Mrs Pearson sobbed. 'It's as if she were here, in this room . . . '

'I don't sound like Penny!' Veronica shouted desperately. 'I don't. Listen.' And she took a deep breath and sang once more: *I'm just a Broadway baby, heading for the heights, waiting for . . . '*

She faltered and fell silent when she saw from their faces that it was Penny's voice that they heard. Her eyes brimmed with tears and she said, 'I'm not Penny. I'm not. I'm me. I sing like *me.*'

And a voice, a voice that she knew and hated so well, sounded in her ears. 'But you don't,' it said. 'You sound like *me*. And you always will. Always.'

'No!' Veronica shouted in terror. She swung round, but saw only the startled face of her mother and Dottie Denver and the other girls. And then the voice came again.

'You fool,' Penny said. 'You stupid fool. Did you really think that you could get rid of me so easily?'

'Yes!' Veronica cried. 'Oh, yes!'

Then Penny laughed, and the sound of her laughter filled Veronica's head until she thought it would burst.

'But you made a mess of it, didn't you?' the voice

went on. 'Just as you always do. No, you didn't get rid of me. I'm *here*. With you. Inside you. And I'm going to stay with you forever.'

'No!' shouted Veronica. 'No! I'm sorry . . . '

'It's too late to be sorry,' said the voice, Penny's voice. 'There's no going back now. You should have thought of that before, shouldn't you?'

Veronica screamed and screamed and screamed until little Miss Spindle, who understood, pushed her way through the others and took Veronica in her arms and cradled her like a baby until the screaming stopped and they took her home.

Lost in France

'We're lost,' said Mrs Blackett. 'We must just face the fact that we're lost.'

Ben had never been to France before, and he didn't think much of it. This was the last straw.

'We're lost,' his mother repeated. 'We are L-O-S-T Lost.'

'Oh, do stop saying that,' Mr Blackett said irritably. 'How *can* we be lost? Here, let me have a look.' He snatched at the map. It ripped neatly right down the middle.

'Very clever, I must say,' sneered Mrs Blackett. 'A torn map is just what we need.'

Mr Blackett opened his mouth, remembered that Ben and Vicky were in the back of the car, and shut it again. He peered at each half of the map in turn, hoping for inspiration.

'That last place was called Moncon-something, if that's any help.' Ben peered over his father's shoulder at the crumpled Michelin. 'The place with the ruined castle.'

'I know, and it *isn't* any help,' his father snapped. 'We're not supposed to be anywhere near there. We're supposed to be over *here*.' He jabbed the map viciously. It split neatly along a crease, and Ben's mother gave a sharp sarcastic laugh.

'There's no need to make things worse,' she said loftily. 'And losing your temper won't help either.'

'I'm not losing my temper!' Mr Blackett shouted.

'Don't raise your voice at me,' Mrs Blackett said coldly.

Ben sighed to himself. There was going to be a scene. He knew the signs.

There had been scenes at regular intervals ever since their journey began. There had been a scene at Southampton, when their elderly Renault refused to start and had to be pushed onto the car ferry. And there had been a scene at Le Havre when the car had to be pushed off. There had been a scene at the garage when his mother insisted that it was her turn to drive, and a scene a few minutes later when she forgot that she was supposed to be on the right-hand side of the road and drove the wrong way round a roundabout. There had been scenes in a restaurant ('Tell him that in England we're used to eating with *clean* knives and forks'), and in the centre of Alençon ('It's not my fault if they hang their silly little traffic lights over the road where no one can see them'). It seemed to Ben that their progress through France had been punctuated by a series of minor explosions.

It was apparent that Mr Blackett had not recognized the alarm signals. 'If you'd been navigating properly, we wouldn't *be* lost,' he said bravely.

Ben held his breath in the silence that followed.

'There was nothing wrong with my navigation,' his mother said at last, in a voice that could slice steel. 'If you'd provided a decent map, there'd be no problem.'

'I still think we should have kept straight on at that last big place. What was it? Chateauwhatsit.'

'The sign was pointing to the right,' said Mrs Blackett.

'Yes, but sometimes that can mean keep straight on.'

Mrs Blackett smiled grimly. 'Well, *I* can hardly be blamed for *that,* can I? It's hardly *my* fault if the French point their signs to the right when they mean straight on.'

There was a pause as they all stared out at the wide rolling landscape. Crickets chattered on the roadside, and a thick blanket of heat settled comfortably on the car.

'Anyway,' Mr Blackett said, not content to let matters rest, '*you* were navigating when we got lost in Le Mans.'

Mrs Blackett waved a dismissive hand. '*Everyone* gets lost in Le Mans,' she said grandly. 'Thelma Prescott says that you've never really *experienced* France unless you've been lost in Le Mans. Preferably in the rush hour.'

Mr Blackett muttered under his breath. Ben couldn't hear what he said, but his mother's ears were sharper. 'If it wasn't for Thelma,' she said, 'we wouldn't be here at all. Just you remember that!'

'I remember it all the time,' Mr Blackett said, and gave a sardonic laugh.

It had all been Thelma Prescott's idea in the first place. She was a friend of Ben's parents—well, a friend of his mother, really, for his father despised their shared enthusiasm for amateur dramatics—and she owned a cottage in France. 'In a delightful village,' she'd told them. 'St Solange-la-Forêt. Miles from anywhere and absolutely *French,* if you know what I mean. The cottage? Oh, an old farmhouse. *Very* quaint but all mod. cons. naturally. *Do* go and stay there. No, you must. I *insist*. We like our friends to make use of it. You'll love it there. Very quiet, of course, but there's so much to see nearby.'

And so they had decided to spend their holiday at Thelma Prescott's cottage in France instead of walking in the Peak District, which is what Mr Blackett would have preferred. But Mrs Blackett felt that France would be better for Ben, who ought to see something of the world whether he liked it or not, and for Vicky, who was doing O-level French and would be able to act as interpreter, and so it was arranged. In the event, Vicky refused point-blank to speak any French at all ('They'll only laugh at me'), and spent most of her time writing postcards to a person called Dennis with whom she claimed to be in love. When she wasn't writing postcards, she stared into space and sang to herself.

'Well, we could hardly leave her at home alone,' Ben's mother had said when he pointed out that Vicky was about as much fun as a kick in the teeth. 'And anyway, travel broadens the mind.'

'Travel will have its work cut out broadening hers,' Ben had observed darkly.

He looked across at Vicky now. She was staring out of the window singing tunelessly to herself, as usual. Something about being lost in France and the day was just beginning.

'Shut up, Vicky,' said their father, peering at the remains of the map. 'I'm trying to work out where we are. Now, *there's* Chateauwhatsit. And *there's* St Solange. So if we keep on, and turn . . . '

'Are we going to sit here all day?' Mrs Blackett asked irritably.

'No, we are not,' said Mr Blackett. 'I am going to get out of the car, open the boot and take out the cheese and bread we bought this morning and a bottle of wine—maybe *both* bottles—and go into that field and have lunch. Then I will get back into the car, and drive on until we get to St Solange and the mythical holiday paradise belonging to Thelma Prescott. Anyone who wishes to join me, can. All right?'

'Sounds okay to me, dad,' Vicky said cheerfully, and clambered out of the car, followed by her father and Ben.

Mrs Blackett opened her mouth to object, and then thought better of it. 'Hang on,' she said. 'Wait for me.'

*

'Now then, what's the name of *this* place?' Mr Blackett said. 'Look out for a sign, someone.'

'There!' shouted Vicky. *'Chaussée déformée.'*

'Don't be ridiculous,' her father snapped. 'That means the road surface is bad.'

'So much for O-level French,' said Ben, and then yelped as Vicky jabbed him in the ribs.

'As if we needed telling, anyway,' said Mrs Blackett darkly. The car had begun to judder and shake on a road that gave every appearance of having been the epicentre of an earthquake.

They had been driving for about an hour since their lunchtime stop, with only a vague idea of where they were going. It didn't seem to matter at first, thanks to the kindly effects of cheese and wine consumed in a poplar-shaded field, but now, as the heat grew more stifling and the journey more interminable, tempers were beginning to fray. They had passed through several villages, each more picturesque and lifeless than the last. None of them had been marked on Mr

Blackett's map, a fact which his wife was only too pleased to point out.

'Does it matter?' he said irritably. 'We're going in the general direction, that's the main thing.'

'We're going in the general direction of *Africa,*' Mrs Blackett said acidly, 'but it doesn't mean that we want to go there. But then,' she added unkindly, 'I don't suppose your map would show *that,* either.'

Mr Blackett ignored her. He peered at the latest village and said plaintively, 'Where are we?'

Then Ben saw the sign. 'St Solange!' he shouted excitedly. 'It says St Solange!'

Even Mrs Blackett joined in the cheering that erupted inside the Renault.

Mr Blackett smiled, and relaxed his grip on the steering wheel. 'I was beginning to think that it didn't exist,' he said happily.

'And what a delightful place,' Mrs Blackett cooed. 'I do think those shutters on all the houses are charming.'

Ben thought that the shutters would look even more charming if they were not so firmly closed over every window in sight, but he didn't say so. Instead, 'We're here at last!' he crowed. 'St Solange-les-Roches.'

'*What?*' shouted his father, and braked suddenly. '*What* did you say?'

Ben looked bewildered. 'St Solange-les-Roches. That's where we are. That's what the sign said.'

Mr Blackett groaned. 'It's the wrong place,' he said.

'What d'you mean?' asked Mrs Blackett. 'How can it be the wrong place?'

'This is St Solange-les-Roches,' he said quietly. 'Thelma Prescott's house is at St Solange-la-Forêt.'

'Oh, nonsense,' said Mrs Blackett, and burrowed in her handbag. 'I've got the address here. Somewhere.

Yes, here we are. "Villa de l'Epine, St Solange . . . " Oh
dear, you're right. "St Solange-la-Forêt. Take the first
turning to the left past the church and follow . . . "
Yes, it definitely says St Solange-la-Forêt.'

'And this is St Solange-les-Roches,' Mr Blackett said
heavily.

'Well, they must be near each other,' said his wife. 'It
stands to reason.'

'Like London, England, and London, Ontario, I
suppose?' Mr Blackett sneered.

Mrs Blackett wisely ignored him. 'We'll ask someone,' she said. 'Drive on into the centre.'

'I think,' said Mr Blackett, 'that this *is* the centre.'

There was silence as the rest of the family stared out
of the car windows. It looked as though Mr Blackett
could be right. The car was parked in a shady square.
There was a cluster of plane trees in the middle with
some benches beneath them, and the inevitable bare
patch of earth where, in other villages they'd passed,
old men in blue overalls and black berets played the
French version of bowls. In this village, though, there
wasn't a single old man to be seen.

'Well, it *is* only half past two,' said Mr Blackett. 'I
expect everyone's asleep.'

'Or dead,' said Ben.

On one side of the square was a pompous building
with a flight of steps in front of it and the sign *Mairie*
over the door. Opposite that stood a church. The
remaining buildings consisted of shops and houses in
various stages of dilapidation.

'Charming!' observed Mrs Blackett. 'Quite charming. So *French!*'

There was no one about. In fact, Ben noticed, there
was no sign of life at all. The houses were all firmly

shuttered, and the half-dozen small shops were closed too. Vicky peered through the car window at a notice on the door of a nearby *boulangerie*.

'*Congé annuel,*' she read. 'Closed for the holidays. Hard luck on anyone here who wants bread. I'm getting out to have a look round.'

'Me too,' said Ben, and followed her out of the car.

Outside, the heat was intense and so, too, was the silence. They stood for a moment, gazing round them, and then Vicky wandered off towards the church. By now, Ben's parents had joined him.

'I'm going to find someone to ask,' said Mr Blackett. 'This is ridiculous. I can't make head or tail of the map.'

'What about me?' asked Mrs Blackett plaintively.

'What do you mean, what about you?' said Mr Blackett. 'You can come with me or stay with the car. It's up to you.'

'I'll stay with the car,' she decided. 'Someone might try to steal it.'

'If they do,' said Ben, 'ask them the way to St Solange-la-Forêt.'

Mrs Blackett glared at him, and climbed back into the car as Mr Blackett walked briskly towards a ramshackle building labelled *Café-Tabac*. Ben watched him for a moment and headed for one of the seats under the trees in the middle of the square. At least it would be cooler there.

Ben sat down and let the stillness fold over him. The village seemed to be totally deserted. The silence was uncanny and Ben shivered. Then suddenly he heard footsteps behind him, and he leaped to his feet and turned round. But it was only Vicky, returning from her expedition to the church.

'It's nice and cool in there,' she said, flopping onto the seat beside him. 'But a bit creepy. Bits of it are falling down. And guess what, there's a stuffed crocodile hanging on a wall. There is really,' she added, as Ben looked at her in disbelief. 'Go and see for yourself if you don't believe me.'

'I believe you, I believe you,' said Ben. 'Anyway, I'm too hot to move,'

'And there's an enormous picture of some bloke being burnt alive by savages. Really gruesome. The Blessed Théophile somebody.' There was a pause as she looked at the square, and then she started to sing to herself again.

'Here's dad,' said Ben after a while. 'I hope he's found someone. I want to get out of this place.'

'It gives me the creeps,' said Vicky, and she moved along the bench to allow their father to sit between them. 'Any luck, dad?'

'No,' panted Mr Blackett. 'I can't find anyone at all. The café's shut. There's a small hotel over there but that's locked too. And all the shops. I couldn't find a police station.'

'What should we do?' asked Vicky.

'Let's drive on,' said Ben. 'Maybe the next place will be better. It may even be on the map.'

'Or we could stay here,' said Mr Blackett. 'Someone's bound to turn up sooner or later. It's a pleasant enough little place. And we've plenty of time. It's not as though we've a train to catch. And St Solange-la-Forêt can't be far.'

'It's so hot,' said Vicky. 'I could do with a drink or something.'

'It's all my fault,' said her father gloomily. 'I should have brought a larger-scale map. But it seemed such a

straightforward route. And Thelma Prescott made it sound so simple.

'I hate Thelma Prescott,' said Ben.

There was silence as they sat together on the seat and waited for something to happen.

Ben was the first to see it. He'd been idly tracing a pattern in the dust with his shoe and when he looked up—there it was. A car. A car had arrived in the square, and was parked quite close to their own. Another car. He hadn't heard it arrive, none of them had, but there it was, just the same. A car. And a car meant people. And people meant help.

'Dad,' he said. 'Do you see what I see?'

His father whistled softly in surprise. 'I knew someone would turn up,' he said. 'Soon be on our way now.' He stood up and looked across the square at the new arrival.

'Funny-looking car,' said Vicky.

'It's an old Morris Traveller,' said Mr Blackett. 'Long time since I've seen one of those. In jolly good nick by the look of it. Someone knows how to care for a car.'

'So the people could be English, then?' asked Ben. 'If it's a Morris?'

'More than likely,' said his father. 'Let's hope they've got a good map.'

They gazed across at the car and, as they watched, a door opened and a man got out, followed by a woman and, a little later, by a boy of about Ben's age. It wasn't all that easy to make them out: the glare from the sun was intense, and the distant figures seemed to shimmer like a mirage.

'There's something odd about them,' said Ben. 'They look . . . '

'It's the clothes,' said Vicky. 'Look at the woman's skirt. And her hair. And those earrings. Years out of date.'

'And that boy's wearing shorts,' said Ben. 'Look how long they are. And his hair . . . '

'I don't know what you're going on about,' Mr Blackett said irritably. 'They're clearly just a rather odd English family. There are plenty of them about, goodness knows. Especially abroad.'

Yes, thought Ben. Like us, for instance.

'But those people look like something out of an old film on television,' objected Vicky.

'Does it matter what they look like?' asked her father. 'All *I* care about is whether they know where they are and where we are.' And he set off purposefully across the square towards the Morris.

By this time Mrs Blackett had noticed the new arrivals, too, and was making her way towards them. The people from the Morris were standing quite still by their car. Ben and Vicky followed more slowly. By the time they reached the Morris, the four adults seemed to be getting along like a house on fire.

'Ah, there you are,' Mrs Blackett said cheerfully when she saw them. Then she turned to the Morris people. 'This is my daughter Victoria, and my son Benjamin. Vicky and Ben for short. And this is Mr and Mrs Johnson and Kenneth. They're from Aylesbury, just imagine! Isn't it a small world? And would you believe it, they know the way to St Solange-la-Forêt. Isn't that tremendous luck!' She beamed happily.

'Yes, we can take you there quite easily,' Mr Johnson said.

Ben stared at him. The man had curious eyes: grey and cold and lifeless. The woman, too. The boy,

Kenneth, stood a little way behind his parents, with his gaze fixed on him. He was small and dark and looked anxious.

'Oh, there's no need for that,' Mr Blackett was saying. 'We don't want to put you to any trouble. Just tell us how to get there, that's all. Draw a map if you like.'

'No,' said Mr Johnson firmly. 'I insist that you let us guide you. Just follow our car. It's no distance, it won't take long.'

'We're going that way ourselves,' the woman said. 'So it will be no trouble.'

'Well, if you're sure . . . ' Mr Blackett said.

'Of course they're sure,' Mrs Blackett said. 'I really do think we should accept Mr Johnson's kind offer, don't you? The sooner we get there, the better. I've had quite enough of this heat. And I'd give my right arm for a cup of tea.' She giggled, and Mr Johnson smiled in reply.

But Mr Blackett wasn't going to be hurried. 'You're familiar with the area, I take it?' he asked.

'We've been here for some time,' Mr Johnson said.

'A lovely part of the world,' Mrs Blackett said. 'We're so looking forward to our stay. If,' and she shot her husband a murderous glare, 'if we ever get there.'

'Oh, you'll get there,' Mr Johnson said.

Ben glanced at the boy, Kenneth. He was still looking straight at Ben and his eyes – his eyes seemed to be signalling an urgent message. Was he trying to tell Ben something? Ben looked at him questioningly, and then Kenneth shook his head urgently and mouthed the word: 'No.'

Ben gaped at him. What on earth could he mean? But

he didn't have time to find out for he heard his mother calling, and turned round.

'Do come on, Ben,' Mrs Blackett said.

He looked quickly back at Kenneth, but he and his parents were clambering into the Morris.

When he reached the car, Ben said to his father, 'Can I sit in the front for a change, dad?'

'If you like,' his father said. 'If your mother doesn't mind.'

'Why should *I* mind?' asked Mrs Blackett. 'Don't bother about me. I'm just the dogsbody who can't navigate properly.'

Mr Blackett sighed loudly, and switched on the engine.

'I don't like those people,' Ben said. 'I don't want to go with them.'

'Why ever not?' asked his father. 'They're only going to lead us to St Solange-la-Forêt. That's all.'

The car lumbered into motion and followed the Morris round the square and down a side turning.

'I don't like them,' said Ben. 'I don't trust them.'

'They *are* a bit odd, I must say,' said his father. 'But they're only guiding us to Thelma Prescott's cottage. We won't see them again after that.'

'Their clothes are amazing,' said Vicky. 'Really Fifties. I wonder where they got them.'

'I think you're all being most unkind,' Mrs Blackett said frostily from the back seat. 'We're lucky enough to meet some people—kind *English* people—who offer to help us when we're lost, and all you can do is criticize them. It's most ungrateful of you.'

By now they had left the village behind, and were driving along a minor road that grew steadily more narrow and more uneven. The ground rose steeply on each side, and gaunt rocky outcrops punctuated the wooded hillsides. The Morris bounced along ahead of them and, every now and then, Kenneth's pale and anxious face would appear at the rear window to stare back at them.

'Funny boy, that,' Mr Blackett said, and then, 'Thelma Prescott didn't say anything about the road being as bad as this. It's little more than a track.'

'I suppose those people *are* trustworthy.' Mrs Blackett sounded doubtful for the first time.

'Well, I can't see why they'd deliberately mislead us,' said Mr Blackett. 'I can't see what they'd gain from it.'

'I don't like it, dad,' Ben said urgently.

'Don't be silly,' his father said. 'There's nothing to worry about.'

Ahead of them, the road veered sharply to the left to skirt a rocky crag, and the Morris trundled briskly out of sight round the bend.

'It's very quiet, isn't it?' said Mrs Blackett. 'We haven't passed any other traffic at all.'

'Hold on to your hats!' Mr Blackett called out cheerfully, as the Renault swung into the curve. And then, as the road straightened out ahead of them once again, he whistled and said, 'Where have they gone?'

'What d'you mean?' Ben asked, peering through the windscreen.

'The Morris,' said his father. 'It's disappeared.'

'It can't have.'

But his father was right. The road in front of them was now completely empty.

'Perhaps it's put on speed and raced ahead,' Ben suggested doubtfully. 'Look, there's another bend coming up.'

Mr Blackett steered the Renault round another crag

and then, as the road straightened once more, Ben let out a shout.

'*Look out!*'

The road ahead was completely blocked by a dark confusion of tumbled rocks, boulders, earth and fallen trees.

Ben shut his eyes as the car hurtled towards the mass of rocks. They were going to crash. He knew that they were going to crash. They'd all be . . . His father twisted the steering wheel desperately, and the car lurched off the road and into a ditch.

Ben heard the engine roaring, and the sound of someone crying in the back seat. He looked out of the window. Steep wooded cliffs towered on each side of the road. If his father had been a fraction of a second slower turning aside, the car would have run straight into the barrier of rocks ahead.

He turned to look at his father. Mr Blackett's hands were trembling on the wheel, and he was breathing heavily.

'Are you all right, dad?' Ben asked anxiously.

'Yes,' his father said. 'Yes, I'm okay. But I don't understand. They led us straight into it. Those people led us straight into it. It's as if they wanted – as if they wanted us to crash.'

'But that's impossible,' said Mrs Blackett. 'They couldn't . . . '

'And where *is* the Morris?' said Ben. 'Where's it gone? What happened to it? What happened to those people?'

It was then that Mrs Blackett started to scream.

*

'I just don't see how you could have gone wrong,' Thelma Prescott said. 'It's so incredibly straightforward. I know it's easy to make mistakes in a foreign country but *really* . . . All you do is take the N10 out of Tours and turn off . . . '

'We did all that,' Mr Blackett said. 'We followed your instructions. But these things happen, don't they?'

Mrs Prescott looked unconvinced. 'And I don't understand why you were on that road at all. It's been closed for years, ever since the landslide happened, oh, well over twenty years ago.'

'There weren't any signs,' Ben said. 'None at all. How were we to know?'

'You might all have been killed,' Thelma said. 'You almost were. And I'm surprised the car came off so lightly.' She got up to pour more tea, and then turned. 'I've just remembered something,' she said. 'An English family were killed in that very spot in, when? Nineteen-fifty something? Their car crashed straight into the rocks and they were all killed. What was their name now? Thompson? Johnson? Something like that. There was a child, I think. Yes, a boy. It was the talk of St Solange for years. They *still* talk about it. And that's why they closed the road. Blocked it off. You have to go the long way round to get to the village now.'

'But there wasn't a barricade,' Ben began, and then stopped as he saw his father's warning glance.

'Still, I hope you were able to enjoy the rest of your holiday,' Thelma said. 'When you eventually got to the cottage.'

'Well no, not really,' said Mrs Blackett. 'Our hearts weren't in it after what had happened. That's why we came home early.'

'What a pity,' Thelma Prescott said. 'You must go again next year.'

'Yes, well, we'll have to think about that, won't we?' Mr Blackett said, and quickly changed the subject.

Ben looked at Vicky. She smiled, and then began to sing to herself, very softly. Something about being lost in France.

Squeal, Piggy, Squeal

As soon as Jane woke up, she knew that it was going to be a bad day. To begin with, it was raining. And to make matters worse, it was the day of her birthday party.

Jane hated birthday parties. She hated any kind of party, but she hated birthday parties most of all. Other people's were bad enough but at those she could always disappear into the loo during the more idiotic games, or say that she felt sick and had to go home. If the worst came to the worst, she could always pretend to faint. She'd done that at Delphine Withers' party, during a particularly stupid game of Musical Spoons, and the entire party had ground to a satisfying halt. Delphine told her bitterly the next day that everyone else had gone home as soon as Jane had been driven away in Mr Withers' Volvo. Jane considered the possibility of fainting at her own party that afternoon, and decided against it. To faint at one birthday party would be regarded as bad luck, but to faint at two might well be seen as evidence of a lingering disease. No, one's own birthday party was a different matter altogether. She would have to stay until the bitter end, and try to look coy when everyone sang, 'Happy Birthday to You.' There was no escaping it.

She got out of bed, and crossed to the window to inspect the weather. If it rained hard enough, there might be a flood and the party would be cancelled. But there seemed to be no possibility of a flood; the rain had already slackened to a depressing drizzle, and a girl who was standing on the other side of the road didn't even look wet. Jane stared at her, and wondered idly what on earth she was doing out there so early in the morning. How very odd, she thought, and then forgot all about her; she had more important things to worry about. The party, for instance.

When Jane went downstairs, she found her mother in the kitchen, busily making custard for a trifle. Her father was there, too, wrapping a bar of chocolate in layer after layer of paper ready for Pass the Parcel. Old Mrs Andrews from next door, who always came in to help on special occasions, was constructing an elaborate gâteau with a tin of pineapple chunks, a packet of digestive biscuits and a plate of grated coconut.

'Look,' said Jane, 'if it's all too much trouble, I don't mind not having a party. Honestly I don't.'

'Don't be silly, dear,' said her mother. 'What would I do with all those chocolate fancies? Not to mention the birthday cake.'

Jane had forgotten the birthday cake. A great slab of soggy grey sponge covered in rock-hard pink icing and ten candles.

'And anyway, everyone's been invited. They'll have bought your presents,' Mrs Tasker added, as if this were all that mattered.

'They could keep the presents for someone else's birthday,' Jane said reasonably. 'And you could give the food to the poor.'

Mr Tasker yelped with laughter. 'Do you know how much we've spent on this party of yours? We're the poor ones now, you know.' He glanced out of the window. 'Looks as though the rain's stopped. I'll go and set up the barbecue when I've finished this.'

Jane had forgotten about the barbecue too. She'd forgotten that no birthday party was complete without her father's special brand of charred hamburger served with underdone sausages under a cloud of foul-smelling black smoke.

'Well, if it's all so expensive, why don't we cancel it?' Jane asked. 'Think of the money you'd save.'

'It's too late for that,' her father said. 'We've bought all those hamburgers, haven't we? And the ice cream. And the crisps. Who'd eat all those crisps if we cancelled your party? And anyway, we don't want to disappoint your friends, do we?'

Jane gave a hollow laugh. 'Friends? They're not my friends,' she said. 'I only invited them because they asked me to *their* rotten parties. You don't honestly think that Delphine Withers is a *friend* of mine, do you?'

'Well,' said Mr Tasker, 'I *did* think . . . '

'She's awful,' Jane went on. 'They're *all* awful. I hate the lot of them. And I don't want this horrible party. I don't want to play those silly games. I *hate* parties.'

She was answered by a terrible silence.

'You can be an awful pig sometimes, Jane,' her mother said at last in a strained voice. 'Of course you want your party. We *all* want your party. It's going to be *such* fun.' Then, 'I'd put some glacé cherries on top, if I were you, Mrs Andrews. Just to finish it off.'

Jane wondered if she'd gone too far, and then decided that she hadn't. 'No, I don't want it!' she shouted. 'You never think about me, or what *I* want. I *don't* want the party! I *don't!*'

'She's over excited,' Mrs Tasker said to no one in particular. 'That's what it is. Over excited.'

'Some people don't deserve treats,' Mrs Andrews said primly, standing back to admire her creation. 'Do you think there's enough meringue in it, Mrs Tasker?'

Mrs Tasker considered. 'Oh yes,' she decided. 'I think that's enough. But perhaps a few more chocolate buttons wouldn't come amiss.'

'*Some* children never have parties,' Mrs Andrews said darkly. 'I could tell a tale or two. I knew a little girl once who never . . . '

'Apples!' said Mrs Tasker suddenly. 'Have we got enough apples?' She disappeared into the larder.

'The poor soul,' Mrs Andrews went on. 'The little girl, I mean, not your mother. *She* never had a birthday party. I expect she'd have done anything to have a birthday party of her . . . '

'Yes, we've got enough,' said Mrs Tasker breathlessly, coming back into the kitchen. 'We mustn't forget Ducking for Apples, must we? Your father always enjoys that game more than anything.'

'He wouldn't if he was the one who had to play it,' Jane said rudely.

'That's enough now,' her mother said sharply. 'If you're not going to make yourself useful, you'd better stay out of the kitchen. We've got a party to get ready whether *you* like it or not. And you might show a bit of gratitude.'

Jane scowled, and retreated quickly into the garden. By now the drizzle had stopped, and pale sunlight was filtering through the clouds. Her father would be pleased: the barbecue could take place without interruption, and it also meant that rain would not stop play in the Treasure Hunt, planned to take place just after tea.

She wandered idly down the side path into the front garden, and then stopped short as she came in view of the road. Someone was standing on the opposite pavement. It was the girl. The girl that Jane had seen earlier from her window. She had straggly fair plaits and was wearing a blue dress and sandals. She was standing perfectly still and staring. Staring straight at Jane.

For a time the two girls stood motionless, each gazing at the other. Then, suddenly, the girl with the fair plaits moved. Without looking to the left or right, she crossed the road and walked up to the gate of Jane's house.

Jane watched the girl in silence. And then she walked down to the gate to meet her. 'Who are you?' she said. 'And what do you want?'

'I used to live here.' The girl spoke in little more than a whisper.

'What's that got to do with me?' Jane asked. 'I couldn't care if you used to live in China.'

'Couldn't you?' said the girl, and there was a pause. Then, 'I want to come to your party,' she said. 'Please invite me to your party.'

Jane couldn't believe her ears. 'You're joking!' she gasped. 'Do you honestly think I'd invite a complete stranger?'

The girl smiled. 'One more won't make any difference. You'll hardly notice I'm there.'

'Oh, I'll notice all right,' said Jane. 'No, you can't come. I don't know you. I don't *want* to know you. And you can't come to my party.' She turned, and ran inside the house, slamming the door behind her.

*

By the time the first guests arrived for the party, Jane had forgotten about the girl with the plaits. And when four o'clock came, and with it Sarah Armstrong clutching a jigsaw puzzle wrapped in bright pink paper, she only had thoughts for the ordeal to come.

Sarah Armstrong was followed by Karen Hunt and Jennifer Staples, and then the trickle of arrivals became a steady stream. Among the last to appear was Delphine Withers, who arrived very grandly in her father's Volvo.

'I nearly couldn't come,' Delphine announced loftily as she thrust a very small present into Jane's hands. 'But I didn't want to let you down.'

Jane opened her mouth to say something rude, but saw her mother's warning glance and thought better of it. Instead she smiled sweetly at Delphine and said, 'Thank you very much. I'm glad you could make it.'

Delphine turned to Mrs Tasker then and said, 'At Jackie Mansfield's party we had a super disco. With a proper D.J.'

'I'm afraid we've nothing like that,' Jane's mother said, looking worried. 'Just the usual games. And a barbecue,' she added brightly.

It was clear that Delphine wasn't impressed. Jane, who knew that the 'proper D.J.' at Jackie Mansfield's party had been her spotty twelve-year-old brother, started to tell her so but was interrupted by the door-bell.

'More guests!' Mrs Tasker chirruped merrily. 'Answer that, will you, Jane dear? I'll just make sure that everything's ship-shape in the galley.'

Jane shot her a glare, and stamped into the hall. She flung open the front door, and gasped. The girl was standing there. The girl with the fair plaits, the blue dress and the sandals.

'Hullo,' the girl said. Her mouth twisted into a cold mocking smile.

Jane stared at her in amazement, unable to believe her eyes or her ears. And then she slammed the door shut in her face. She stood for a moment, breathless with anger and surprise. How dared she? How dared she ring the bell and expect to be invited in? Who did she think she was? Who was she?

And then the bell rang again. It rang. And rang. And rang.

Jane stayed where she was, listening to the persistent chime, knowing who would be waiting on the other side of the door.

'Aren't you going to open it?'

Jane turned. Delphine Withers was standing behind her, looking puzzled.

'Yes – no – I mean, yes,' Jane mumbled. And then, 'No, *you* open it.'

Delphine looked at her as if she were mad, shrugged and reached for the door handle. The door swung open, and Jane shut her eyes. She waited for Delphine's surprised greeting, and the girl's whispered reply.

'It's nothing to get excited about,' Delphine said. 'It's only Tony Ralli,' and Jane opened her eyes to see not the stare of the girl with plaits but the bewildered face of the boy who lived next door but one.

When Jane returned to the sitting room, the party was well under way. Her father had divided the children into two teams, and a rather listless balloon race was taking place. Jane was happily too late to take part, but she couldn't avoid the game which followed.

'How about Grandmother's Footsteps?' Mr Tasker suggested brightly.

No one showed much enthusiasm for this idea, and Delphine Withers muttered, 'Aren't we a bit old for this sort of thing?'

'No one's too old to enjoy themselves,' Mr Tasker said pompously. 'We could play Squeal, Piggy, Squeal instead, if you like.'

'When Carol Rosen had *her* birthday we all went roller skating,' Delphine said loudly. 'And then we went to the Chinese take-away afterwards.'

'I hate Chinese food,' said Jennifer Staples, and Jane shot her a grateful glance.

'Carol Rosen's a pain in the neck,' added Giles Murphy.

Delphine glared at him. 'You only say that because you weren't invited.'

'Drop dead, fat face,' said Giles.

Delphine's lip began to tremble, and Mr Tasker said

quickly, 'Now then, that's enough of that. We'll play Squeal, Piggy, Squeal. Who's going to go first?'

Jane sighed and put up her hand. 'Me, I suppose,' she said. 'Seeing that it's my party.'

'Good girl!' said Mr Tasker heartily. 'Now you all know the rules, don't you?'

'No,' lied Delphine Withers.

'Well, everyone sits in a circle,' Mr Tasker began. 'And then we put Jane—or whoever it is— in the middle, and we blindfold her—or whoever it is. Then we spin her round, and she has to find her way to the edge of the circle and touch one of you. Then she sits in that person's lap and says, "Squeal, Piggy, Squeal." And then that person has to squeal like a pig in a disguised voice, and Jane has to guess who you are. And if she guesses right, you change places with her,' he finished triumphantly.

'I didn't understand a word of that,' said Delphine Withers.

'Well, you'll see as we go along,' said Mr Tasker. 'Now then, get into your circle. And we'll blindfold Jane and put her in the middle.'

It took some time for everyone to form a circle, but at last it was done, and Jane stepped unwillingly into the centre. She scowled at Delphine Withers as she waited for her father to turn his handkerchief into a blindfold.

'I hope you don't sit on *me,* Jane Tasker,' Delphine said nastily. 'Not until you've lost some weight.'

'Don't worry, I won't come anywhere near you,' said Jane. 'I'll be able to tell where you are by the smell.'

'Here we are,' said Mr Tasker then. 'Sorry to keep you waiting. Ready, Jane?'

Jane nodded, and snatched a final glance at the circle of expectant faces. And then, in the last moment before the blindfold covered her eyes, Jane saw her. She was there, sitting with the others. Grinning with the others. The girl with the plaits. The girl with the cold blue eyes.

'No!' Jane shouted, tugging at the blindfold. 'No, she *can't!*'

'What's the matter?' Her father pulled the handkerchief free and looked at her anxiously. 'What's wrong, Jane?'

'That girl!' Jane shouted. 'Get rid of her! She shouldn't be here. I didn't invite her!'

There was complete silence in the room, and Jane was uncomfortably aware that everyone was staring at her open-mouthed. They must think she was mad. Perhaps she was. For she could see quite clearly now that the girl wasn't there. She wasn't there at all. Any more.

'Which girl?' her father asked. 'What do you mean?'

'The girl with the plaits,' Jane said feebly. 'The girl with the plaits and the blue dress. She was sitting *there.*' She pointed, and then she dropped her hand quickly when she saw how much it was trembling. She hoped that no one else had noticed.

'But there's no one here with plaits and a blue dress,' Mr Tasker said. 'There never was.'

Someone giggled loudly.

'I know,' said Jane. She could see that for herself. 'I must – I must have imagined it.'

But the girl *had* been there. Jane had seen her. She was there. At the party. In the house. Somewhere.

Jane pushed past her father and ran out of the sitting-room into the hall. There was no sign of the girl there. She rushed upstairs but the bedrooms were empty. She came downstairs again and burst into the kitchen where her mother and Mrs Andrews looked up in surprise.

'What's the matter, dear?' her mother asked. 'Playing Hide and Seek?'

'I'm – I'm looking for – have you seen a girl?' Jane panted. 'A girl with fair plaits and a blue dress?'

Mrs Tasker shook her head. Mrs Andrews said, 'Fair plaits? That's funny.'

Jane stared at her. 'What do you mean—funny?'

'Well,' said the old lady. 'That girl who lived here years ago. The one who never had parties. Funny little thing, she was. *She* had plaits, fair plaits. I wonder what happened to her.'

'Well, she isn't in *here,*' Mrs Tasker said briskly. 'Now, are you all ready for tea yet?'

'I'll go and find out,' Jane said, and walked slowly back to the sitting room.

There was an embarrassed silence when she went in, which was broken by her father. 'Ah, there you are,' he said, rubbing his hands. 'Welcome back! You're just in time to duck for apples. I've got everything here.'

'Tea's ready when we are,' Jane said, hoping this news would distract him. She loathed ducking for apples.

'Good,' he said. 'Now then, who's going to duck first?'

'I will,' said Giles Murphy.

Karen followed Giles, and then Tony, who annoyed Mr Tasker by deliberately splashing Delphine Withers. Then came the shout that Jane expected and dreaded: 'Come on, Jane! Where's the birthday girl?'

Jane stepped forward and knelt by the old tin bath that her father kept especially for this annual ritual.

'Hands behind your back,' Mr Tasker said. 'Now then. Let's see how well you can do.'

Jane stared at the water and at the gleaming apples bobbing on the surface. Oh well, she thought. Better get it over with. And she lowered her face to the water.

And then, suddenly, someone seized her shoulders so tightly that she cried out, and a voice, a voice she knew, *her* voice, hissed in her ears: 'It's our game now, Jane. You didn't go through with the last one, did you? But we'll play now, shall we? The two of us. Yes, we'll play it now.'

Jane could hear her father's voice, too, but his sounded strangely distant. 'Come on, Jane,' he was saying. 'What are you waiting for?'

And then louder, closer, came the cold insistent whisper of the girl in plaits, and the grip on her shoulders tightened.

'Yes, we'll play now. Come on, piggy. Squeal, piggy. Squeal, piggy, squeal!'

And then someone pushed Jane's head down and under the water. She struggled to get up, but the hands were too strong for her. Her mouth opened in a scream, but the sound was stifled by water. She fought against the hands and against the choking darkness, but she could not move, and there was a roaring in her ears that grew louder and louder and then blackness . . .

'Jane! Are you all right? Jane!'

Jane opened her eyes and blinked at the brightness of the room. Her hair and face were soaking wet. She was lying on the carpet, and her father and the others were looking down at her anxiously. She struggled to get up but her father said, 'No, lie still for a moment. What happened? Did you faint?'

'She . . . someone tried to drown me,' Jane muttered. 'She pushed my head under the water. I couldn't breathe . . . '

'No one tried to drown you, love,' her father said. 'That's what I don't understand. You put your head right under the water. You were struggling and kicking but – but you kept your head right under. You wouldn't lift it. Why?'

'I *couldn't!*' Jane screamed. 'Don't you see? I couldn't. She was drowning me.' She sat up and stared wildly at the others. 'She was, I tell you. She *was!*'

'But Jane,' Delphine Withers said gently. 'There was no one there. No one was drowning you, I swear it. There was no one there.'

*

Later, when the other children had gone home and the uneaten food had been tidily tucked away in the larder and the fridge, Jane wandered out into the garden. The girl with the fair plaits, the blue dress and the sandals was waiting by the gate, as she had expected. But Jane was too tired to be frightened this time. And besides, the party was over.

'It was all your own fault, you know,' the girl said. 'Everything would have been so much easier if you'd invited me properly in the first place. There wouldn't have been any fuss. No unpleasantness. No one would have noticed anything wrong. But now?' She shrugged her thin shoulders. 'Still, you'll know better next time, won't you?'

'Next time?' asked Jane, and her stomach lurched with fear.

'Yes, next time,' said the girl. 'Next year. Your next birthday party. You will invite me next time, won't

you? I know you won't forget. I would so hate to miss
it.'

And the girl with the plaits smiled a thin, cold smile.
And disappeared.

A Nasty Piece of Work

When I came home from football that Tuesday and my mother told me that we'd been invited next door for the evening, I nearly hit the roof.

'Both of us?' I asked, hoping against hope that she was joking.

'Both of us,' my mother said firmly. 'And that means you, sunshine. So get upstairs and wash that ugly mug of yours, and while you're about it find something to wear that doesn't look as though you've slept in it for a month.'

I groaned, and pretended that I'd forgotten how to climb the stairs.

'Get a move on,' my mother said. 'We're late as it is.'

'I'm dying,' I croaked, clutching the bannister feebly. 'I've got a mortal disease. Don't make me go next door, please! Anything but that! Anything!'

'*Martin!*'

Her voice had that sharp edge to it which always meant that the joking had to stop, and I scuttled obediently upstairs.

I hated going next door. Not that it happened very often, for my mother didn't really get on with the Adamsons. We exchanged visits occasionally, just to be friendly, but that was about as far as it went. And I didn't really get on with their spotty son. I didn't have much to do with him at school, either, even though we were in the same form. Oliver Adamson was the sort of boy who was always on his own, not because he was unpopular but because he just kept himself to himself. But his parents and my mother seemed to think that we ought to be friends, simply because we lived next door to each other and were more or less the same age. It was dotty, really. No one expected *them* to swear undying friendship just because they were the same age and lived next door to one another. So why did they expect it of us?

I tried to explain this to my mother when I went downstairs in the cleanest shirt I could find, but I didn't make much headway.

'I really don't know what you're going on about,' she said. 'And why are you wearing that disgusting shirt?'

'Because all the rest are even more disgusting,' I said. 'Thanks to your total inability to look after me properly.'

'Well, you can't go to the Adamsons looking like that. They'll report me to the authorities and have you taken away.'

'I doubt it,' I replied. 'I tried reporting you myself but they wouldn't believe me. Shall I put on the one I was wearing before?'

'No. You may as well keep that one on. If you sit in a dark corner maybe no one will notice.'

'There is *one* solution,' I said gleefully. 'I can stay at home and then it won't matter *what* my shirt looks like.'

'*Martin!*' The sharp edge again.

There was a pause while she peered at her reflection in the hall mirror and then she turned back to me.

'Look,' she said, 'I know it's not much fun going to the Adamsons. I don't want to go, either. That's why I need you with me, for moral support. Okay?'

I nodded, and then flinched as she planted a kiss on my forehead.

The Adamsons' house was identical to ours, but it couldn't have been more different inside. Ours was littered with overdue library books, old magazines, unironed shirts and elderly dog biscuits, while the Adamsons' was tidy and clean and extremely boring. I knew which one I preferred, but I wasn't too sure about my mother sometimes. I caught her giving their sitting room an envious look as we waited for Mr Adamson to bring her a glass of wine.

'Don't worry,' I whispered. 'I bet they piled all their dirty washing into the back room just before we came.'

She smiled at me, and then twisted her mouth into a frenzied social grin as Mr Adamson came in with our drinks.

'Everyone happy?' he asked jovially and then, without waiting for an answer, 'That's the ticket.' He sat down, took a gulp from his own glass, and went on, 'Beryl will be along as soon as she's finished the tea things. We're running a bit late tonight. Because of the washing machine.'

'Ah, yes,' my mother said, pretending to know what he meant.

Mr Adamson's beady gaze alighted on me then and he said, 'Oliver's up in his room, Martin. You know where it is, I expect.'

I sighed and got to my feet. Here we go. Send the little boy out to play. I winked at my mother as I went out, and she grinned back.

I paused in the hall and wondered what would

happen if I walked straight out of the front door and back to our house. None of the Adamsons would even notice I'd gone, but my mother would. Better not, then. I headed for the stairs instead.

Oliver's bedroom door was closed. I wondered whether I was expected to knock, but it was only Oliver Adamson's bedroom, after all, not the headmaster's study. On the other hand, I couldn't just barge in. In the end I decided on a compromise: 'Oliver!' I called. 'It's me, Martin Fox.'

The door opened and Oliver peered out. His black hair was tousled as usual. 'Oh,' he said. 'It's you.'

'Yes,' I said. 'Sorry about that. Can't be helped, I'm afraid.'

Oliver looked at me with contempt. 'You'd better come in,' he said at last. 'I suppose.'

I gasped when I saw his room. The last time I was there it had been festooned with model aeroplanes, and every available flat surface had been littered with bits of balsa wood and glue and all the other materials needed to construct more. Now, all the planes had disappeared. Instead, the walls had been painted bright red, and were dotted with pictures and drawings of witches and monsters and bats. I peered at a drawing of a vicious-looking giant fly and shuddered.

'That's the demon Beelzebub,' Oliver said cheerfully. 'The lord of the flies.'

'Yuk,' I said. 'I hate flies. And what's *that?*'

'Oh, that's supposed to be a photograph of a real werewolf.'

'Looks more like a dead dachshund to me.' I was trying to be funny, but Oliver didn't laugh. 'Don't tell me you actually *sleep* in here?'

Oliver looked offended. 'Of course I do. But,' a grin

flashed across his pale face, 'my mother won't set foot in the place.'

'Can't say I blame her,' I said. 'You must be out of your tiny mind.'

Oliver scowled at me, and then looked away. 'None of your business,' he muttered, and I suppose he was right.

I wandered round the room for a bit, looking at the pictures. There was one of a severed human hand, green and wrinkled and gruesome.

Oliver perked up when he saw me looking at that. 'It's a hand of glory,' he said. 'It was cut from a hanged man, and pickled and dried.'

'Oh, do shut up,' I said.

'No, it's true,' Oliver went on. 'If you set the finger tips on fire, you could open locked doors and stop sleeping people from waking up. Burglars used them a lot.'

'I bet they did,' I said drily. 'Do you expect me to believe all that?'

'It's true!' Oliver said indignantly. 'If you don't believe me, look in those books.' He pointed to his desk, and to a pile of books lying on top of it. One of them was called *Magic, Witchcraft and Ghosts*.

'You take all this stuff seriously, then?' I asked. 'You believe it all?'

'Of course.' Oliver suddenly bent down and dragged a tin box from under his bed. Then he looked up at me anxiously. 'If I show you my museum, promise you won't tell anyone?'

'Your museum?'

'I – I've been collecting things,' Oliver said. 'Unusual things.'

'Instead of model aeroplanes?'

'I grew out of *those* ages ago,' he said scornfully. 'No, these things are much more exciting.'

'Let's have a look, then,' I said. 'I won't tell anyone. Promise.'

At first glance, Oliver's tin box seemed to be filled with dirty stones and old bottles but, as he lifted each object out, it became clear that there was much more to them than that.

'This is a witch stone,' Oliver said, showing me a pebble with a hole in it. 'It protects the wearer against witchcraft.'

'Handy,' I said, and picked up a little bottle which seemed to be filled with black earth.

'That's bats' blood,' Oliver said carelessly.

'Oh, is that all?' I said. 'I should have known.'

He ignored me. 'You can use it for various things— magic charms, love potions. And,' he lowered his voice

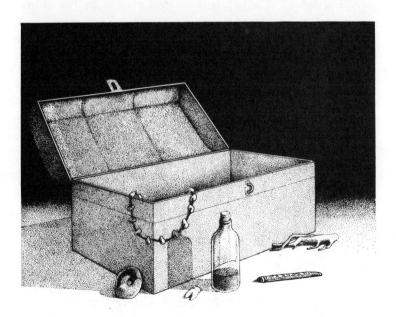

to a whisper, 'it's part of a recipe for flying ointment.'

I burst out laughing then. Oliver was furious, but I couldn't help it. Flying ointment! Did he really expect me to believe all that?

It seemed that he did. He snatched the bottle from me, replaced it in the box and slammed the lid. 'It's no laughing matter,' he said grimly.

'I'm sorry,' I spluttered. 'I really am. Show me the rest. Please.'

Oliver looked at me for a moment, and then relented. He opened the box again.

'What's that necklace for?' I asked, peering inside.

'It's a protection against the evil eye.'

'And that thing that looks like a carrot with legs?'

'It's not a *carrot,*' Oliver said indignantly. 'It's a mandrake root. They scream when they're pulled out of the ground, and if you hear them you die or go mad.'

'Charming!' I said, and rooted round in the box. 'Hey, this looks like a tooth.'

'It is,' said Oliver. 'It's a dead man's tooth. If you wear it round your neck you don't get toothache. You're really supposed to bite it out of the dead man's skull yourself if it's going to be really effective.'

'Does this one work?' I asked.

'Of course,' he said. 'I haven't had toothache since I got it so it must be. And look,' he went on, holding up a small yellow tube that looked like a carved cigarette holder that someone had trodden on, 'this is a witch stick. It's a test of belief in witchcraft and all that sort of thing. If someone has this in their possession, and they don't believe in witchcraft, then the stick sends out horrible ghosts and demons to haunt them.'

'Well, don't give it to me, then,' I said. 'I think this is all a load of rubbish. And I think you're nuts.'

Oliver gave me a long cold look. Then he put the witch stick back in the box and lowered the lid. 'I knew you'd say that,' he said at last. 'I knew it was a mistake to show you these things. I should have kept quiet about them.'

'Tell you what,' I said wickedly. 'You could prove me wrong, couldn't you?'

'What d'you mean?' Oliver was looking interested now.

'Well,' I went on, 'I admit that I don't believe in bats' blood and screaming carrots and things. So why don't you make something happen? To prove that they work.'

'Cast a spell, you mean?'

I shrugged my shoulders. 'I dunno. Just do something to prove that — that magic or whatever it is really works. That's all.'

'What sort of something?' Oliver asked, his eyes shining.

I thought desperately. 'Do something to someone,' I said. 'Make someone ill. Someone like – like – like Miss Webster.'

Miss Webster taught French. She had dark untidy hair and a face like a horse. I couldn't stand her. And she couldn't stand me.

'Okay,' Oliver said. 'I'll do it.'

'Oh.' I was taken aback by his swift acceptance of the idea. 'When? And how?'

'Soon,' Oliver said vaguely. 'And I won't tell you how. I can't. It wouldn't work if I did. But I'll do it, all right. I'll prove it to you.'

'Oh, good,' I said nervously, wondering if I'd set something in motion that I'd live to regret. But no, how could I? It was all nonsense.

We both went downstairs after that and joined my mother and Oliver's parents in the sitting room. They were talking nineteen to the dozen, but I could tell that only sheer determination and several glasses of wine had kept my mother going through the ordeal. We said good-bye as soon as we could.

Oliver followed me down to their front gate when we left.

'Don't forget,' I said.

'I won't,' he grinned. 'You'll get your proof. Don't worry.' And he turned and went quickly back into the house.

As we walked the few yards to our own gate, my mother said curiously, 'And what was all that about? It sounded very cloak-and-dagger.'

'Oh, nothing much,' I said carelessly. 'That Oliver's a nasty piece of work, if you ask me. He's a nut case.'

My mother started to laugh then, but I didn't. I felt uneasy. 'It's not funny,' I said. 'He really does give me the creeps.' And I remembered Oliver's intense eyes, and how serious his voice had been when he said that it was no laughing matter.

I found it hard to get to sleep that night. I kept remembering those pictures in Oliver's room. The bats. Snout-nosed demons in hell. The grinning goat mask over his bed. And the giant fly, Beelzebub. Then, when at last I slept, I dreamed that I was chased by a severed hand with fingers aflame.

*

I didn't give Oliver or his magic claptrap another thought until the following afternoon when the bell rang at the end of English, and I realized that the next period was French. It was only then that I remembered

Oliver and his red bedroom and my challenge. I swivelled round in my desk. He always sat in a back corner of the classroom, tucked well out of harm's way. And there he was as usual, his black hair tousled and his eyes dark. He saw me looking at him and smiled mysteriously.

The bell rang for the start of French, but Miss Webster didn't appear. She was rarely late, unlike old Mr Thompson, who taught Geography and often forgot to turn up at all for his lessons. And then, at last, the classroom door opened and Mrs Walters, the deputy head, rushed in, looking flustered.

'All right, quiet now,' she said, as a curious buzz rose in the room. 'There's nothing to get excited about. I'm afraid that Miss Webster's had an accident. Nothing too serious, I'm glad to say,' she went on, raising her voice to be heard over the excited yelps of the front row girls, 'but she won't be coming to school for a few days.'

Janice Macklin stuck her hand in the air. 'What happened to her, miss?'

'As I said, nothing to worry about,' said Mrs Walters. 'She had a nasty fall on her bicycle and she's broken her ankle. That's all. I'm sure some of you have done the same thing.'

'I broke my arm last year, miss,' Janice Macklin said smugly.

'Oh, really?' Mrs Walters looked as though she was fighting the temptation to break Janice's other arm there and then. 'Now, Miss Webster hasn't forgotten about you, and she's asked me to set you some work . . .'

I stopped listening to Mrs Walters and turned round to look at Oliver. His eyes met mine, and he smiled.

' . . . and I hope that you took all that down, Martin Fox, because I'm not going to repeat it just for your benefit.'

I realized that Mrs Walters was talking to me, and I turned back to face her. 'Yes, miss, no, miss,' I said. But I couldn't think about her or about French. All I could think of was Miss Webster, and her broken ankle that was all my fault.

*

Oliver was a long time coming out of school that day, probably because he knew that I'd be waiting for him. I usually walked home with Pete Freeman but I told him that I had to talk to Mrs Walters about something. Well, I don't think that he would have understood my reason for waiting to see Oliver Adamson after school. And I wasn't prepared to tell him. Not yet, any-way.

'Ah, there you are,' said Oliver, when he saw me.

'Yeah, here I am,' I said. 'All right, I'm impressed. I really am.'

Oliver smirked. 'I told you I'd prove it, didn't I? And I did.'

I hated to see him so pleased with himself. 'Maybe it was a coincidence,' I said slowly. 'Maybe old Webster would have fallen off her bike anyway. I bet it had nothing to do with your rotten magic.'

He shrugged. 'You'll have to take my word for it, won't you?'

We walked on for a while in silence. Then, 'Tell me how you did it,' I said craftily. 'Go on. Tell me.'

Oliver shook his head. 'I can't.'

'Why not?'

'It's against the rules.'

We had stopped to wait for traffic lights to change. 'What rules?' I asked.

'There are special ways of doing things,' he said mysteriously. 'I can't tell you any more than that.'

We crossed the road and started to climb the hill towards the turning where we lived.

'Course you can,' I said. 'You can tell *me*.' When he didn't reply, I went on, 'I won't tell anyone, I promise. Cross my heart and hope to die, etcetera.'

'I just said some words,' he muttered.

'What words?'

'Oh, just – just words. That's all.'

I started to laugh. I couldn't help it. Here we were, two schoolboys walking home along a shady suburban road, and one of them was claiming to have injured a teacher by saying a few magic words. It was incredible. Unbelievable. What kind of a fool did he think I was?

'You're having me on,' I told him. 'I don't believe a word of it.'

'Please yourself.' He shrugged his shoulders again.

We walked on. Oliver was lying. He had to be. No one in his right mind could believe all that nonsense. I certainly didn't. Of course I didn't. Did I?

By now we had reached Oliver's front gate. He stopped, and smiled at me. 'You really don't believe it, do you?' he said. 'You don't believe in magic.'

I shook my head. 'Course I don't.'

'Well, then,' he said, 'you won't mind borrowing the witch stick, will you? For one night. Just to make sure.'

I stared at him. What on earth was he talking about?

'In my museum,' he went on. 'The small carved stick.'

'Oh, yes,' I said. 'The stick that sends out demons to haunt you if you don't believe in it.'

'That's the one. Well, then. Why don't you take it home with you?'

I didn't know what to say, 'Well, I – um – I'm not sure – ' I stammered feebly.

'You won't have anything to worry about,' Oliver said. 'If you're right and the magic isn't true, then the stick is harmless. Useless. Nothing will happen.'

'And if I'm wrong, and it *is* true?'

Oliver gave me a mocking smile, and I felt an urgent desire to smash his silly face in.

'Give me the stick,' I said quickly. 'I'm not scared of it.'

'Hang on a minute, then.' And he ran through the gate and up the path to the house.

As I waited for him, I wished, not for the first time, that I'd kept my stupid mouth shut. I didn't want to get involved with Oliver Adamson and his crazy ideas. But then I didn't want him to think that I believed all that rubbish about ghosts and demons. I didn't want him to think that I was scared of a silly little carved stick.

It wasn't long before Oliver came running down the path again. 'Here it is,' he said, and thrust the stick into my hand.

I looked at it. It was dull yellow, about eight centimetres long, and carved with an intricate design that was impossible to decipher. It still looked like a cigarette holder that someone had trodden on. I quickly put it in my pocket, and started to walk away.

'I'll come and collect it first thing tomorrow,' Oliver said. 'I can't wait to hear about the ghosts.'

'You'll be wasting your time,' I said, turning to look back at him.

Oliver laughed. 'Will I?' he said. 'Will I?'

He laughed again and went back inside the house, leaving me gaping on the pavement.

*

I stayed up as late as I possibly could that night. Luckily one of my mother's favourite old films was being shown on television, and I was able to sit and watch it with her. It was a stupid old British film about two people who meet on a railway station, but I wasn't able to concentrate on the story. All I could think of was Oliver's jeering face and the small yellow stick in the pocket of my blazer upstairs.

The film ended at last, and my mother sniffed loudly into her handkerchief. 'It always makes me cry,' she said. 'They don't make films like that any more.'

'Thank goodness,' I muttered darkly.

'All right, you,' she snapped. 'High time you climbed up the little wooden hill to your little wooden bed. In other words, beat it, wise guy.'

'Can't I have a cup of coffee or something?' I pleaded. Anything to delay going to bed. But what was I afraid of? Nothing. Nothing at all.

'A cup of cocoa, then?' I said, when my mother shook her head at my first suggestion.

'Bedtime, Martin.'

'How about a nice glass of warm milk?'

'*Martin!*'

I admitted defeat then and went upstairs, switching on every light as I went. I didn't believe a word that Oliver had said, but I wasn't taking any chances. I closed the bedroom door behind me and then changed my mind and left it open. Then I got into bed and waited. I felt drowsy after a while, but when I shut my eyes all I could think of was Oliver's jeering face and Miss Webster's broken ankle.

I suppose I must have fallen asleep because the first thing I remember after that is opening my eyes with a start. I stared into the darkness, my heart pounding, and then I relaxed. A fly was buzzing in the corner of the room. Just a fly. The noise must have woken me up.

I lay back, and closed my eyes again. But the buzzing went on and on, and as I listened another fly joined it over by the window. And then, unbelievably, yet another started up by the bed.

I groaned loudly, and wondered whether I should wait for the flies to fall asleep, or whether I should get up and find something to swat them with. It was warm in bed and cold out of it, so I decided to stay where I was.

The buzzing went on. It sounded as though more flies had joined the chorus: the noise grew louder and more insistent, and seemed to be coming at me from all sides. Then one of the flies swooped down at my face and bounced off my cheek. I lashed out angrily with my hand, and I think I must have hit it for it started to buzz in the desperate, angry way that they do when they've been wounded.

Other flies began to swoop round my head then, and for the first time I felt uneasy. The room seemed suddenly to be filled with angry insects. They were buzzing on all sides, and every now and then one of them would swoop down at me, brushing my face with its bristly little body. I lashed out again, flailing my arms like a madman, and sent my bedside lamp crashing to the floor. I reached down and put it back on the table, and switched it on. Nothing happened. The bulb had gone.

I wondered what to do next. The buzzing was growing louder and louder, as if an entire orchestra of flies was filtering into the room. Where were they coming from? The window. It must be the window.

Flinging the bedclothes aside, I leaped out of bed and ran to the window. I closed it, and then ran back to the haven of my bed. Flies bounced against my legs as I ran, and one or two met an untimely end beneath my bare feet. I scrambled back between the sheets and covered my face with the bedclothes.

The noise stopped then, blotted out by the welcoming silent warmth of the bed. But then I heard buzzing again, and felt the tickling, bristly touch of flies on my bare ankles, my wrists, my face. They were in the bed. There were flies in the bed.

I shouted, and scrabbled desperately at the bedclothes, trying to brush the flies away. I could see them in the faint moonlight that was shining through the window, a mass of scurrying black smuts on the whiteness of the sheets.

I jumped out of bed, and as I did so the buzzing grew even louder, and flies dived at me from all directions, bouncing off my arms, legs and chest, and crawling over my face. They were everywhere. I opened my mouth to shout, and a fly crawled inside, wriggling and itching and buzzing. I retched, and scooped it desperately away. Then I sank down beside my bed with my arms covering my head.

Suddenly I felt calmer. I could still hear the dreadful buzzing, and I could feel the tiny bodies brushing my hair, my legs, my hands, but I didn't feel frightened any more. I would stay where I was and wait for the flies to go, or to fall asleep, or whatever it was that flies did. I would keep calm. I wouldn't panic.

And then, as I waited and listened, the buzzing seemed to grow softer, as if, one by one, the flies were growing tired. The noise became more erratic, and fewer flies than before swooped around my head or landed on my feet and hands. Perhaps they were giving up at last.

And then there was silence. The flies had stopped. They had gone. Slowly, oh, so slowly, I lifted my head to look.

As I looked up, the noise started again. Buzzing, as loud as road drills, filled the room, and the air was thick once again with the small flying bodies. But there was something else there now. Something large and looming that seemed to fill the room. And there was a smell, and a horrifying sucking sound.

I peered into the darkness at the shape and the noise and the smell. And I saw two enormous eyes, two vast, winking, flashing globes, and beneath them two huge feelers, and long jointed legs covered in thick stubbly hairs, and two gigantic wings that shimmered in the moonlight.

I think I screamed then. I know that I leaped to my feet and ran. I ran through the storm of flies and out of the room, pulling the door closed behind me. I ran downstairs, sobbing and moaning, and lay down at last on the sofa in the sitting-room.

*

'Come on, sleeping beauty. Wake up, you'll be late.'

I opened my eyes and blinked. It was morning, and my mother was looking down at me.

'What on earth are you doing here?' she asked. 'Why aren't you in bed?'

I remembered then what had happened the night

before. Remembered that I was on the sitting-room sofa.

'I – I – I don't know,' I stammered. 'Perhaps I walked in my sleep. Don't ask me.' I sank back on the cushions and tried hard not to remember.

'Well, you'll be late if you don't watch it,' said my mother. 'Oh, and Oliver Adamson's here to see you.' She gave me a puzzled stare. 'Funny time to call. I didn't realize you were such good friends.'

'We're not,' I mumbled. 'Believe me, we're not.'

'Well, he's here,' my mother said.

She went out of the room, and then, shortly after that, Oliver appeared in the doorway. 'Well?' he said.

'Well, what?'

'Did anything happen? Any ghosts? Demons?'

'No,' I said. 'Nothing happened at all. I don't know what you're talking about.'

'Oh.' He smiled. I'd expected him to be disappointed, and wondered why he wasn't.

'Remind me to let you have your stick back,' I said.

'Oh, don't bother,' he said. 'It's only an old cigarette holder of my mother's. I trod on it a bit to make it look old.'

I stared at him blankly. I didn't know what to say.

'I fooled you, didn't I?' Oliver said. 'You really believed it.'

'No,' I croaked. 'I didn't. 'Course I didn't. I'm not that stupid.' There was a pause. Then, 'What about the bats' blood?' I asked. 'And the dead man's tooth?'

'Oh, that was just an old bottle I found in a field,' Oliver said carelessly, 'with earth in it. And the tooth was mine. Look.' He pulled open his mouth, but I shuddered and looked quickly away. 'And the mandrake root was a funny-shaped parsnip,' he went on.

'That's all.'

'It was all lies?' I asked.

Oliver nodded. 'Just a joke.'

'And Miss Webster's ankle?'

He laughed out loud. 'A coincidence,' he chuckled. 'Just a fantastic coincidence.'

'Yeah, fantastic,' I muttered. He really was a nasty piece of work. 'What if I don't believe you?' I went on.

He looked blank. 'What d'you mean?'

'Well, you say you were lying before. How do I know you're telling the truth now?'

Oliver gave me a sly smile. 'You don't, do you? It's for you to decide.' He looked at me scornfully for a moment, and then moved towards the door. 'Well, that's that, then. Just thought I'd check. I'm glad you didn't see any ghosts or anything.' And he giggled. 'See you around.'

'Not if I can help it,' I mumbled as he turned to go.

And then, suddenly, my mother appeared in the doorway, her eyes wide with alarm. 'Martin . . . ' she began, and then stopped when she saw Oliver.

'What's up?' I asked.

She shrugged her shoulders and said, 'I'm not sure. I don't know.'

'What do you mean?'

'I've just been up to your room,' my mother said. 'And there are flies everywhere. Hundreds of them. Dead flies. On the bed, the carpet, everywhere. The room is filled with dead flies.'

I stared at her, and Oliver turned and smiled at me. A long mocking smile.

'Where did they come from?' my mother asked. 'All those flies. Where did they come from?'

'I don't know,' I said. 'I just don't know.'